THE DEATH DETECTIVE AND THE SKELETON

In Southfield, when a skeleton with a ligature around its neck is unearthed by a hungry fox, the Death Detective, DI Essach Wangdula, is brought in to investigate. The Detective Inspector is Sherlock Holmes's descendant; his assistant is DS Flora L. Hughes. Identification of the body by facial reconstruction leads the pair to London where they learn that the victim had been involved in a suspicious death. Then another body is discovered in Southfield and it's reported that there are now two missing people. Suddenly, Wangdula knows that he's up against a committed serial killer.

JOHN F. RICE

THE DEATH DETECTIVE AND THE SKELETON

Complete and Unabridged

ULVERSCROFT
Leicester

First published in Great Britain in 2011 by
Robert Hale Limited
London

First Large Print Edition
published 2012
by arrangement with
Robert Hale Limited
London

British Library CIP Data

Rice, John F.
The death detective and the skeleton.
1. Detective and mystery stories.
2. Large type books.
I. Title
823.9'2–dc23

ISBN 978–1–4448–1319–7

Published by
F. A. Thorpe (Publishing)
Anstey, Leicestershire

Set by Words & Graphics Ltd.
Anstey, Leicestershire
Printed and bound in Great Britain by
T. J. International Ltd., Padstow, Cornwall

This book is printed on acid-free paper

Dedication

Matthew Cheese: PC Technician,
Church Stretton
Thank you for sharing your
expertise with me

1

She'd already tangled with Adrian Hill and had found out how strong he was and just how fast his reactions were. He'd somehow snatched her right arm behind her back and ejected her from her former home. She was not about to repeat that error, and had only done so because, at six feet four inches tall and muscular, she'd thought herself a match for any man. She judged Adrian Hill to be about two inches shorter than her. He was lean and obviously very fit. Perhaps he had to be physically fit to do his job.

A car came along the road towards the porch where she had concealed herself. She'd perched her bottom on the brick dado on one side of the porch, the better to remain hidden while she peered above the dado wall on the opposite side. She crouched lower as the car's headlights momentarily illuminated her hiding place. The smell of bad eggs from the catalytic converter made her instantly think of Adrian Hill. He's a bad egg — and worse, a blackmailer. He'd discovered how she'd carried out her last murder. It was now essential that he die before next Friday's payment, and there were only six days left in which to kill him.

Because she could not stand the sight of blood, she would strangle him, just as she'd strangled her husband seven years ago.

She'd realized then that a strangler had to be significantly stronger than the victim to overcome resistance. Otherwise resistance had to be overcome by the element of surprise, or drugging, or knocking the victim unconscious first. In her husband's case she'd got him so drunk that he'd passed out. He'd been a giant of a man, nearly as tall as she, and dangerously strong. She'd thoroughly enjoyed throttling him with her bare hands until he'd stopped choking and breathing. Afterwards, garden twine, tightened around his neck, had ensured he'd never revive. Nobody would ever find his body, she'd made sure of that. The same must happen to Adrian Hill. He would have to be killed using the element of surprise; she intended to first knock him unconscious.

Then she saw him. A street light further along the road momentarily illuminated his face and his unmistakable walk as he passed beneath it. Pulling her shoulders in she made herself as small as possible to condense her tall but shapely body.

The envelope sent to her former home and

redirected via her solicitors, contained a photograph of the item which would undoubtedly incriminate her. On the back were the words, 'Meet me in Ealing Broadway shopping centre square at twelve noon, Saturday. I know how it was done.' That was when the blackmail had begun.

By discreetly following Adrian Hill from his place of work she'd been able to find out where he lived and to study some of his habits.

She had learned that the chartered surveyor gambled and that he visited his local every Saturday night before returning home to watch late night TV. He had not, so far, taken anyone back to his flat. She was glad that he was alone.

This Saturday was to be her opportunity. Clad all in black, including balaclava, gloves and trainers, she knew she was all but invisible, crouching in the deep porch of the house with the 'For Sale' board in the front garden. Running her forefinger around the front of her balaclava she made sure no stray blonde hair had escaped. She was inappropriately dressed for a June night and felt perspiration trickle between her breasts and down her stomach and back. The thin crescent moon gave off very little light and the amber street lights did not penetrate to where she hid. She clutched her mallet in readiness.

She allowed Adrian Hill to pass the front garden gateway. Then she moved swiftly and silently to get behind him. The last thing she needed was for him to pass under the next street lamp and see an extra shadow on the paving. Perhaps Adrian Hill sensed movement; he was just turning his head when she brought the rubber mallet crashing down on his skull with all her strength. Her victim lurched before collapsing onto the pavement. She swiftly dragged his inert body back into the porch of the empty house and there, manually strangled him. The same rush of adrenalin she'd experienced when she'd killed her husband coursed through her veins again.

Listening for any sound of breathing she eventually released her grip and removed her gloves. Reaching into her black trouser pocket, she took out a length of garden twine and made a slip knot in it. She looped it around Adrian's neck and tightened it with all her strength so that it disappeared into the flesh, and then she reef-knotted it firmly into place.

Taking a deep breath she willed herself to calm down before searching her victim's pockets and removing money and keys. She carefully checked that there was no one about before opening the boot of her car. Hauling Adrian's body into a sitting position with his front to her, she stooped and swiftly lifted him over her right shoulder. She carried him the few yards to her car parked in shadow. She drooped to allow his body to gently come to rest on the floor of the boot, just as if he were a bag of cement. Pushing at his arms and legs, she folded Adrian's body into the foetal position to fit the confined space.

Removing her balaclava, she recovered her breath, before collecting an electric torch she always kept in her glovebox for emergencies. She walked the short distance to Adrian's flat, pulling her gloves on again as she went. Using the two keys she'd removed from his pocket she quietly opened the front door and let herself into the ground floor flat. Shielding the light from her torch she set about closing curtains without knocking into furniture.

Switching lights on, she looked around her at the disorder which revealed that Adrian had lived in, what estate agents described as, 'a relaxed lifestyle'. How could anyone tell if the flat was burgled? Ignoring the musty smell of dirty clothing, she found a suitcase and filled it with clean clothing, shoes, toiletries and personal items.

His car keys lay on the top of the bedside cabinet. She caught her breath as she found a wad of notes in the drawer. Her money. Although glad to find it she could not help hissing with annoyance at how little of it remained. Gambled away she surmised. But the item she had murdered Adrian for was nowhere to be found. Such a small thing would be capable of being hidden almost anywhere.

She saw Adrian's laptop and placed it in the suitcase before pressing the snap locks home. Perhaps it would reveal where her blackmailer had hidden it. She bared her teeth in annoyance and then brightened at the thought that, with Adrian Hill dead, anyone finding the evidence would never realize its significance, anyway. Picking up the suitcase and, leaving the lights on, she left the key in the lock of the open door as she left the flat.

She put the suitcase on the back seat of her own car. Then she went to Adrian's car and removed the aluminium sectional ladder, and sturdy black plastic case containing the tools of her victim's licit profession, from the boot. She then opened all the car windows and left the key in the ignition. Hopefully, an opportunist car thief would find it and do them both a favour. She added the ladder and tool case to the suitcase on the back seat of her car.

She headed home. She would strip the body before rigor mortis set in and then get the best night's sleep she'd enjoyed in ages. Tomorrow she would cut up the ladder and other tools of the late Adrian Hill's profession. Tomorrow night she would bury his body miles away where it would never be found. The day after, she would unobtrusively dump destroyed clothes and tools at the local council refuse tip.

Satisfaction welled up inside; she felt her mood of hatred lifting, to be replaced with one of near happiness.

Adrian Hill was her fifth murder victim. With the other four, his would become her fifth undetected killing.

2

Detective Inspector Essach Wangdula's gaze surveyed Southfield Park, and was amazed that such a relic of Victorian times could have survived into the twenty-first century, in private ownership.

He imagined that it must have been a haven of peace, before the M40 was constructed less than three miles away, on the south side of Baluster. The sweet smell of new-mown grass permeated his nostrils, and his thoughts were interrupted by a blackbird tut-tutting in the nearby shrubbery, emulating the sound of a senior citizen, whose even tenor of life has been disturbed.

A member of the SOCO team handed him a package, and then he remembered why he was here.

The detective quickly slipped into the plastic trousers, jacket and hat of regulation protective clothing, obligatory at a crime scene. He then pulled on sturdy paper overshoes, latex gloves and a face mask.

A police constable raised the blue and white plastic strip to allow the detective to stoop and enter the shrubbery. Two trestle-like frames supporting low-hanging shiny-leaved rhodo-dendron branches formed a bower in the shrubbery. A blackbird exited noisily as Essach carefully avoided treading on the scattering of dusty soil and small bones, before entering the bower. He found to his surprise that even at his height of six feet he was just able to stand upright in the shrubbery. Criss-crossed branches supported the green canopy. Essach Wangdula peered over the shoulder of the divisional forensic pathologist. Someone had dug there, or more likely an animal starting a burrow, and revealed a human skeleton, scattering the soil and small bones in the process.

'Detective Inspector Essach Wangdula,' he said, by way of introduction.

The voice of the pathologist muffled by his face mask said, 'Your first case here, Detective Inspector Wangdula? You missed the divisional doctor. He confirms that the skeleton is dead,' he added drily, and chuckled. 'Anyway, an interesting job for you, Essach. He wasn't killed here. Just buried in a shallow grave.'

'Hm. Male, you say. How was he killed?'

For answer, the pathologist placed the brush he was using to remove soil from the skeleton to indicate a ligature which had been tied around the neck.

'Strangled. Manually. See the hyoid bone? Snapped in two by strong hands around his throat. In my opinion the ligature was added later.'

'That's odd,' remarked the detective.

'Belt and braces, old chap. Making doubly certain that the victim was dead.'

'Any clothing, body jewellery, a wallet with his name and address in it?'

The pathologist rose to his feet spluttering with laughter. He held out his gloved hand to DI Wangdula. 'Colin. I'll let you know when I've dug deeper. Ah! Here comes the divisional photographer.'

They moved out of the shrubbery to let him pass. The pathologist pulled his face mask down and lodged it beneath his chin; the detective followed suit.

'The neck, Phil. And showing the foetal position. And look above you. I want a shot of that too, please.'

Essach watched as Phil took shots of the skeleton from different angles, and then of the pencil stub caught in the leafy canopy above.

'Sir?'

'Yes, constable.'

'Mr MacMahon, the head gardener, would like a word with you.' He indicated a man standing nearby.

The detective removed his face mask altogether and shoved it into the waistband of his over-trousers. He went to the blue and white tape marking the crime scene area where a man, who Essach judged to be in his early sixties, stood; his brown corduroy trousers, green open-necked shirt and stout leather boots indicated his profession.

'Mr MacMahon, I'm Detective Inspector Wangdula. What can I do for you? I'm in charge of this investigation.'

'We need access to mow the lawn here.'

'I'm sorry, Mr MacMahon,' the detective pointed to finger bones in the grass with a marker beside each one.

'Not a problem', replied Mr MacMahon. 'We can throw those back into the shrubbery where the fox dug them out. We can then all of us get on with our respective jobs.'

Essach Wangdula took a deep breath. Tact. 'I'm sorry, Mr MacMahon. This is a suspicious death. Might even be the scene of a crime. If so, scenes of crime officers will have to scour the whole of this area for possible clues.'

'Pah! He or she was murdered. Go and look, man. Gardening twine around the neck. Been throttled.'

'You are, of course, right, but even so, I can't give you access to mow the grass until

11

after my team have finished their work here.'

The head gardener narrowed his eyes to match Wangdula's oriental eyes. 'This afternoon?'

The detective gulped. 'Tomorrow. By the next day at the latest.' Before the head gardener could turn the look of disgust on his face into an expletive, he added, 'You are right about it being murder but how do you know it is garden twine around the neck?'

'I've seen enough in my job, haven't I? We use it all the time.' With that he turned to his assistant. 'You'd better put the mower away and edge the grass around the flower beds.' He walked away from the detective, calling over his shoulder, 'If you need me I'll be in my office writing up my incident book.'

Waiting until the head gardener was out of sight, Essach Wangdula said to the constable, 'Quick. Before he comes back. Help me extend the cordon just in case he decides to mow this lawn before we've finished.'

The SOCO team erected a screen to conceal the skeleton in readiness for them to carefully excavate it. Flashes from the shrubbery told the detective that Phil was taking more photographs.

After the photographer had finished, the pathologist led the way back into the shrubbery, followed by Essach. They examined the pencil, caught in the upper branches of the rhododendron, without touching it.

'I reckon that could be human hair holding the pencil stub in place.'

The detective drew himself up to his full height. 'I'm six foot and can just stand upright beneath it. For a pencil to have been caught in that branch, surely the only explanation must be that it was lodged behind someone's ear, the person who buried the corpse, and that person must be very tall!'

'Six feet six inches tall?' The pathologist raised his eyebrows in query.

'Hopefully, it will yield some DNA. Someone has chewed it.'

'Hm. I noticed the teeth marks. However, it has probably been here several years, so don't hold your breath.'

Essach Wangdula left the SOCO team to it, stripped off his crime scene protective clothing and went exploring. He followed the path until it forked. He took the right-hand path where it led to a gate with both a substantial deadlock and a padlock and chain securing it. He then retraced his steps until he came to the fork where he took the other path. The sound of sparrows squabbling came from a tall conifer hedge at the end of the path. He went through the archway in the hedge and found himself in a concealed area of brick buildings and greenhouses. He walked across the yard to a door marked 'Head gardener', and knocked.

3

A familiar voice gruffly announced, 'Enter. Mr Wangdula! Come to disrupt my life again, have you? Well, since you're here, take a seat.'

The detective sat opposite the head gardener with an old-fashioned partner desk between them. He peered at the large plan on the right-hand wall, inscribed, 'Southfield Private Park', framed and behind protective perspex.

Mr MacMahon rose, went to it and pointed, 'That's where your skeleton was found. In that shrubbery.' He returned to his seat.

The detective continued to look. 'I see that there are only two entrances to the park. I used the main entrance to get in and found the second one before coming here. It was padlocked.'

'Only at the request of your constable. To keep the residents of Southfield out until you are done.'

'How did you find the skeleton, Mr MacMahon? What drew your attention to it?'

'Before mowing lawns we do a quick check that there are no stones on the grass which could damage the mower blades. We saw the soil heaped up beneath the rhododendron and overspill onto the grass. And then we saw the side of the skull and the twine. It was then we telephoned the police.'

'You mentioned an incident book, Mr MacMahon. Did the finding of the skeleton trigger some memory of an entry in it?'

Mr MacMahon opened his desk drawer and took out a leather-bound book. 'Goes back to 1931.' He flipped through the pages. 'Not an awful lot to report but this could be of help to you. I've often wondered about it. It happened just about two years ago. Here it is. Look.' He placed the opened book in front of the detective.

17 June. The chain securing the Mickleton Drive gate was cut through during last night. There were no break-ins to this office, other buildings or greenhouses, and nothing was found to be missing. The gate deadlock was secured. We assumed that we had had an attempted break-in.

'Or,' the detective mused, 'if there had been an intruder, he could have had a key. He or they could have locked the gate behind them.'

'All keys are accounted for. They're special. We have to send away to Chubbs for replacements.'

'Even so, someone could have used one.

Do you have a record of keys that are reported lost?'

For answer, Mr MacMahon took another leather-bound book from a drawer in his desk and pushed it beside the incident book.

Essach Wangdula flipped through the pages and sighed, 'I see what you mean when you say that all keys are accounted for. But that's not really so, is it Mr MacMahon? Admittedly some keys have been returned to you after the lost one has turned up, but I bet others have turned up and remain unreported. There could be households which have accumulated two keys. Who is to know if the second has not fallen into unscrupulous hands?' He rubbed his chin reflectively. 'Every householder in Southfield will have to be questioned.'

'If you say so, Mr Wangdula.' The head gardener cocked his head questioningly. 'Does that make every householder a potential suspect?'

'Well . . . technically . . . yes.'

The head gardener snorted. 'You'll no be verra popular when the bigwigs around here realize that property prices are about to fall again.' He saw the detective's bewilderment. 'A dead body dumped in the park shrubbery. A murdered body! Everyone a suspect! Property prices hereabouts plummeted after the M40 noise first disturbed the peace. Trees muffle the sounds now. However, you, Mr Wangdula, are just about t'upset the peaceful life in Southfield. You'll no be welcome anywhere here at all.'

The detective felt a chill run down his spine. He recalled the advice of Superintendent Salmone as he appointed him to be the investigating officer. 'Do use tact,' he'd said. 'Please be tactful. There's money in Southfield. And where there's money there is influence and contacts to people with power. In life it is not only what you know but, more importantly, who you know. Do your job but please do it pleasantly and diplomatically. Keep a low profile.'

Essach Wangdula groaned inwardly. 'It would be difficult to get into the park without a key?'

'Virtually impossible. High walls topped with broken glass? Chains with padlocks secure the two gates at night to which only I have the keys.' The head gardener waited for the detective to digest this information. 'And, as you now know, every gate key is accounted for as far as it is possible to check.'

'Show me the two entrances on the map, Mr MacMahon.'

'The main gate is here, off Humphry Drive. My wife and I live in the lodge beside it. The other is here,' he pointed, 'off Mickleton Drive.'

'Nearer to where the skeleton was buried than from the main gate.'

'Oh ay,' the head gardener conceded. 'The skeleton is in this shrubbery.' He pointed it out on the map.

'So it is certain that for someone to have gained access they must have had a key. At what time are the gates locked, Mr MacMahon?'

'At dusk, unless of course, there is a night-time concert. On those occasions the Mickleton Drive gate is padlocked, leaving the Humphry Drive gate as the only way in and out. Attendance is more easily monitored that way.'

'Your incident book entry pins down the most likely date when the body was brought into the park, 17 June, two years ago.' The detective examined the wall plan of the park and surrounding houses.

The head gardener followed his gaze. 'Enough rear gardens about the park, but the body wasn't pushed over the wall of one of those; we'd have found damage to shrubs. Whoever buried that body, well it would have been a body then, came through the Mickleton Gate.'

'I suppose you couldn't find me a copy?'

19

the detective tapped on the perspex protecting the map.

'It'll have to be photocopied in sections and taped together.'

'That'll do very nicely, thank you. Oh! And could you put a cross approximately where the skeleton was found, please? Red would show up well.' Essach Wangdula studied the map taking particular note of the surrounding roads, and then sat down. 'Tell me a bit about the park, and who has access to it.'

'Does the name Humphry Repton mean anything to you, Mr Wangdula?'

The detective shook his head.

'Well now, he was a landscape gardener working in the late eighteenth and early nineteenth centuries. He designed the gardens of Southfield Hall. The hall belonged to the Lloynd-Hunns who died out in the 1890s. The hall was demolished and the land redeveloped, together with the surrounding farm land, with top quality houses. This parkland was retained for a carriage drive from Mickleton Gate to Humphry Drive, for summer open-air concerts, and for nannies to wheel their perambulators. A bygone age, Mr Wangdula! Every householder has t'pay an annual charge towards the upkeep of the park. In return, every householder has a key to gain

20

access to it. It fits both gates,' he explained.

Detective Inspector Essach Wangdula made his way back towards the crime scene. When he saw that SOCOs were still at their meticulous work he sat on a nearby bench. He would wait for them to finish, just in case he was needed.

He watched the SOCO team clearing up. The skeleton had been removed for forensic examination. Essach wondered what his ancestor, the first Essach, the great consulting detective who had visited Tibet over a century ago, would have thought of modern day methods of crime detection.

A constable was left to guard the site, in case further examination was found to be needed. Essach followed the SOCO team out of the park.

4

Superintendent Salmone listened attentively as Essach Wangdula explained the probability of why the murderer, or murderers, must be local from the circumstantial evidence of a key having been necessary to enter Southfield private park after closing hours. Also from the choice of shrubbery used to conceal the body, now reduced to a skeleton, as yet unidentified.

'I shall need assistance in carrying out a house-to-house, in Southfield, sometime soon.'

Superintendent Salmone paled. 'I can spare one detective sergeant. Detective Sergeant Flora Hughes. She is good at her job. Keen. Attentive to detail. Tactful. Yes, tactful. Most important that. Tactful.'

'No constables, sir?'

'Too risky. Residents of Southfield take offence at the slightest excuse. They would feel slighted if anyone less than a detective were to question them. No. No constables. When Detective Sergeant Hughes returns from her present assignment I'll introduce her to you and assign her to this case.'

Back in his office Detective Inspector Essach Wangdula recalled his car ride around Southfield. Large houses with 'In' and 'Out' drives. Some still with their original 'Tradesmen Entrance' and 'No Hawkers or Circulars' signs on a front pillar. If the murderer lived in one of those houses then their eventual discovery would undoubtedly cause a stir in social circles. The victim could also have lived nearby. A feeling like an icy finger ran down Essach's spine. He definitely would have to use tact if his reputation was to remain intact.

★　★　★

On his way home that evening, Essach stopped at the supermarket nearest his police section house flat. His temporary home. He placed a portion of salmon in his basket. He knew that he had frozen peas and some new potatoes in the flat. He added a bunch of pinks to his basket, and a copy of the *Baluster Post* and then went to the checkout.

The first thing that Essach did when he entered the flat was to pick up Rowena's photograph, place a kiss on the glass and arrange the pinks in a vase beside it. His handling of the flowers had released their spicy smell. He added water to the vase, and

23

then carefully watered Rowena's small collection of begonias. Living contacts with her. They made him feel less lonely.

After Essach had eaten his meal he sat in an easy chair and absorbed the local news reported in the *Baluster Post*. He tried to find estate agents' house advertisements but found only two private advertisers. He underlined their telephone numbers, and then ringed the several estate agents' advertisements offering their services. Essach made himself a mug of instant coffee, and then telephoned the two private advertisers. He asked the first what price they were asking. On their reply that they would first like him to view the property, Essach apologized for wasting their time and rang off. They were trying to waste his time, but he was trying, whoever he dealt with, to be tactful. The second advertiser was asking over £200,000. Essach explained that he could not afford that much.

He washed up his meal dishes, saucepans and mug before taking his laptop out of its soft covering. He booted up and typed in the first estate agent's website. Essach scrolled down the list of houses. The prices started at a little over £200,000 and progressively went higher. He did the same with the next, and the next. Finally, he came to Morels. The first house on their list was priced at £120,000. 'Detached cottage, three bedrooms, oil-fired central heating, side garage.' Essach entered the site's video of the property. It all looked clean as each room was panned. Modernish fittings, secondary glazing and early possession. No address was given. Essach frowned, sighed and left a message on the estate agent's telephone service that he was interested in the first property advertised on their website, the one priced at £120,000. He left his mobile telephone number and asked for an evening call.

5

Opening the file on his computer, Essach Wangdula looked at the photographs of the skeleton. Twenty-four hours had passed. Reports from the pathologist lay on his desk. His first problem was to find out the identity of the victim. Only then would real progress be possible in finding the murderer or murderers.

Opening the first report, he agreed with the pathologist's opinion that the body had been folded into the foetal position to transport it in a confined space. An ordinary car boot? The report confirmed that the victim was male, caucasian and gave the probable height of the victim at about 186 cm, and weight at about 80 kg. Colin had thoughtfully included imperial measurement at about six feet one inch, and weight at twelve and a half stones. There were no distinguishing features, no history of broken bones, no deformities. The condition of the teeth suggested that the victim had been in his thirties.

He switched to the report on the pencil stub. He agreed with the pathologist's opinion that it had probably been carried behind one of the murderer's ears, and that it had got caught up in a twig of the rhododendron when the body was being buried. He was particularly interested to read that, *The pencil stub was entangled in human hair probably of a natural chestnut colour, but bleached with hydrogen peroxide, and its length and DNA indicates that it was from a woman.*

Not many women would be strong enough to carry a dead-weight of twelve and a half stones. There must have been two of them, Wangdula surmised. The report continued: *Dental records are being explored. DNA samples from the victim will be placed on the national register in the hope of a match. Similarly, DNA samples taken from the hair which trapped the pencil, will be placed on the National Register in the hope of a match. Endeavours will be made to obtain DNA from the pencil stub which shows signs of having been chewed. The knot in the twine is being examined by an expert in the hope of giving up information. A sample taken from the twine is returned for you to further your inquiries, but it appears to be of a type in common use. The pencil stub is in the hands of an expert and, because of its curious flat lead, should yield some useful information. All reports will be forwarded to you as soon as available.*

Essach Wangdula phoned the pathologist. 'Colin? Thanks for your report. I've read it through. Male. Caucasian. It puts us all into perspective when I read such a simple statement.'

'We're all nothing more than water and a handful of chemicals, Essach. It is how that water and chemical composition is put together that is important.'

'And who put it together?'

'Mm,' came the pathologist's noncommittal reply.

'You are certain that he was manually strangled?'

'The hyoid bone was snapped in two. Strong hands had strangled him to death. The hyoid bone is the only one in the human body that is not attached to another bone. It is delicate. Situated just beneath the chin. You can imagine what happens to it when hands press it from both sides.'

'But the ligature?'

'I think that was put around the victim's neck after he was dead. Probably just to make sure he was dead. Unless, of course . . . '

'Of course of what, Colin?'

'Unless it had a symbolic meaning. Like the Thuggees of India.'

'Ah,' replied Essach, 'a ritual killing.

Perhaps that's why it was not removed?'

'Perhaps. On the other hand the ligature is not very big, and it is my opinion that probably it could have been pulled so tightly that it was embedded in the flesh, so making it difficult to remove. Certainly not without cutting into the flesh.'

'A bit of a bloody job, that! The head gardener has convincing evidence that the body could have been buried during June two years ago. Does that fit in with your opinion of how long the skeleton has been in the ground?'

'That's about right. That surely must help with you tracking him down in the National missing persons register. If all else fails, then get a computer image of the skull and how his face would have looked, and ask the media to publish it in the newspapers and on television.'

6

That evening, Essach received a call on his mobile. 'Frank Morel here, Mr Wangdula. You are interested in our bargain property, The Cottage.'

'Yes, Mr Morel. What's the address, please?'

'You'll probably need directions to find it.'

'Oh.'

'Where are you living now, Mr Wangdula? Which district?'

'Monument Heath.'

'Ah, well. You are not too far away from it. Do you know the railway crossing on Lords Wood Road as you go out of Baluster towards Warwick?'

'No. I've only recently moved to Baluster, but I can use my A to Z. I'll soon find it.'

'Good man. Proceed northwards along Lords Wood Road. Just short of the railway crossing turn sharp left, and The Cottage is about fifty yards on the right-hand side. Can one of my staff meet you there? Show you round. I'm sure that you will be impressed by what is on offer. Very good value for the asking price.'

Between them they arranged a viewing convenient to Essach.

Since his transfer from the Metropolitan Police division he'd lived in a police section house flat in Monument Heath. The limited accommodation was not to his liking. He and Rowena had had their own rented home, a one-bedroom flat with a balcony overlooking quite a large garden, for London properties. With both of them working they had begun saving for a deposit on their own home. And then Rowena had died. Because of the unhappy associations connected to the flat, Essach had moved out. On his parent's insistence, he'd returned to their accommodation above the shop in Acton. When his parents had sold their Oriental Emporium business to retire to India, Essach had requested a transfer away from London.

He needed to start life afresh, and when offered Baluster, had accepted with enthusiasm. His love for his parents had impelled him to give up his home with them, so that the whole property would be vacant. The business premises could then be sold with full vacant possession, resulting in a better price, to boost his parents' retirement income. Out of the proceeds, Essach's parents had given him £100,000 with which to buy his own home.

Someone had told him that houses and flats north of London, were cheaper to buy than similar ones in the metropolis. But Baluster was a dormitory town to London and easily accessible to the capital by rail and road. Consequently, house prices were higher than he'd expected. Having looked at every estate agent's housing list in Baluster, looked on the Internet and the *Baluster Post* advertisements for vendors selling privately, Essach had found just this one house at a price which he could afford with the help of a small mortgage. He might even be able to negotiate a lower price.

★ ★ ★

A constable with several files and reports was distributing them around the open-plan, airy and light, office. The air conditioning was already circulating cool draughts. Another hot day, with the promise to be stifling without an air cooling system. All the detectives had shed their jackets and were working in shirt sleeves. A report was placed on Essach's desk beside his copy of the *Baluster Post*, now his regular newspaper.

'Ah, the ligature report!' Essach pounced on the report and took in its contents: *The ligature is a tightly-made plait of three* strands of a popular common garden twine. It was originally green but has faded to a brown colour. One strand of this particular twine is capable of being broken with a sharp tug. The use of a plaited ligature suggests that this murder was premeditated. The type of knot used is a type of slip knot, which locks tight when pulled into position and is near impossible to undo. It is the type of knot popularly used on packaging in department stores, in nurseries for grafting trees and by carpenters to secure wood joints or fractured timber while glue is setting.

Essach had just enough time to consider the contents of the report when the same constable placed another report in front of him. It contained information on the pencil stub. From it he learned that it was known as a carpenter's pencil. Instead of the graphite core being the usual round shape, it was oblong. Therefore, it was customary to sharpen it to a chisel edge, rather than the more usual point. This type of pencil was commonly used by architects, draughtsmen and some tradesmen including builders and carpenters. Teeth marks had been noted at the top end of the pencil and it was, at present, undergoing tests for DNA. However, the laboratory technician was not very hopeful of success due to the exposure to weather over a prolonged period of time.

Just then the intercom on his desk rang. Essach answered it to hear Superintendent Salmone's voice requesting him to come to his office.

'Let me introduce you. Detective Inspector Wangdula, this is Detective Sergeant Hughes, one of our very best undercover officers. DS Hughes, this is DI Wangdula, lately of the Met, who has established a reputation for himself in solving murders.'

As they shook hands, Essach Wangdula noted the faded denim jeans, peculiar sandals and tightly-fitting beige T-shirt. DS Hughes's long brown hair came to rest on both shoulders. Her brown eyes regarded Essach guardedly.

'DS Hughes has just completed her present assignment, with suitable arrests, I might add.' Turning towards her, Superintendent Salmone said, 'Well done, DS Hughes. I am now redeploying you especially to assist DI Wangdula on house-to-house inquiries in Southfield, with regard to the skeleton unearthed in the private park there. I need hardly remind you both that tact is of the utmost importance when questioning house-holders in Southfield.'

'Yes, sir,' they replied in unison.

Before Essach could ask the question, DS

Hughes had the answer, 'Your desk.'

They sat a respectful distance apart as Essach explained what had been found at the scene-of-crime and showed DS Hughes the reports, and his own notes. While she was reading them, another report was placed in front of Essach. 'Ah, the report on the hair entangled around the twig and holding the pencil stub.'

He read: *The human hair which had trapped the pencil stub to the twig was bleached blonde with hydrogen peroxide and had originally been a shade of auburn. Several hairs range between 28 and 30 centimetres in length. It has provided a DNA reading which reveals that it belonged to a caucasian female. From the position of the pencil stub trapped in the shrubbery (see attached photograph) it had probably become entangled because the pencil stub had been carried behind an ear.*

Essach slid the report in front of DS Hughes. 'All we need now is the forensic report on the skeleton and we might get somewhere in identifying the victim. I'll phone the forensic scientist while you read this latest report.'

'Hello, Essach Wangdula here. Any progress with our skeleton?'

'We have DNA and have sent off for a

search of the national DNA register. There are no indications which might help you find out his identity. There is no history of broken bones apart from the hyoid bone. And we found no trace of anything in the surrounding soil which might lead to ascertaining his identity. His skull could be sent to an expert for a computer image to be created. Pictures from the result could be circulated in the media. He could be shown with and without hair; with a moustache perhaps, and with or without a beard. I'll let you know just as soon as any result comes back from the DNA register or from dental records.'

'Thank you.'

Essach relayed to DS Hughes all that the forensic scientist had told him. They decided on a plan of action. Using the detective inspector's A to Z they divided the roads in Southfield between them. They would begin making their house-to-house inquiries, beginning that evening.

7

Essach and Flora, now on first name terms, spent half an hour in the Hunn Hotel lounge amongst the well-heeled locals. Over Essach's orange juice and Flora's half-pint of dry cider they discussed their interviews of the evening.

'Some of them were helpful but some not. All of them seemed to be glad to see the back of me,' said Essach resignedly.

'Same with me,' remarked Flora, 'with the exception of one who accused the local police force of not doing their job.'

'Oh yes?'

'Reckoned they didn't do enough to track down his aunt's housekeeper when his aunt died under suspicious circumstances and,' Flora paused for effect, '£350,000 went missing.'

Essach couldn't help letting out a low whistle. 'That's a lot of money.'

'Anyway, when I asked if there had been an inquest the nephew admitted that, from the medical evidence, it was determined that his aunt had died from a heart attack.'

'Not a suspicious death?'

'No. His aunt had a history of heart problems.'

'And the money?'

'He inherited his aunt's house and so decided to live there and sell his own house. Reckons he's found where his aunt hid the money but there was no trace of it. And he reckons the housekeeper stole it.'

'A bit of a wild accusation, don't you think?'

'That's what I told him,' Flora explained, 'he showed me the door and said, 'I was just like the rest of them'.'

They departed separately in their own cars. As he drove to his lodgings, Essach couldn't help admiring how Flora was dressed that evening — a smart navy-blue suit and white blouse. What a contrast between her clothing when they met earlier that day! He always wore a charcoal-grey suit, a green shirt with miniature compass cufflinks and a dark green tie. Essach's oriental features precluded him from merging into the background in all but the very unusual undercover operation. His speciality was solving murders and a suit was more appropriate for him to wear on a daily basis.

★ ★ ★

On the following day, Essach and Flora travelled in Essach's car to visit Mr MacMahon. After parking the car, they stayed in it until a brief shower of rain had passed.

They stopped at the shrubbery where the skeleton had lain undisturbed for the last two years. Essach shrugged when they realized that the efficient head gardener had had all signs of the find removed; the visible soil beneath the rhododendron had been raked smooth. They walked on to find him in his office.

'Och! You again, Mr Wangdula.'

Essach introduced his colleague.

'You'll be wanting this.' Mr MacMahon picked up a roll of sheets of paper stuck together with transparent tape. 'The plan of the park you requested, Mr Wangdula.'

'Thanks.' The DI pointed to the plan of the park, now with visible creases, and restored to its place beneath the perspex in the frame affixed to the wall. DS Hughes nodded her understanding. They rolled the copy plan flat on the head gardener's desk. 'Could you put a mark where the body was found and to indicate the two gates, please?'

For answer Mr MacMahon produced a red felt tip and put a cross by each.

'That's the gate where the security chain was cut through, and where, it is obvious, the body, as it then was, was brought into the park.'

While DS Hughes re-rolled the plan, DI Wangdula, asked, 'Found the animal yet, Mr MacMahon? The one that dug up the skeleton?'

'I'm told there was a fox seen asleep on a flat roof of one of the houses just over the perimeter wall. Possibly the culprit, but I suspect it was another fox pushed over the wall of the park by the local nurseryman.'

Essach frowned.

'There is a running feud between us and the nurseryman, and not of my making. Southfield resident's committee, in their greed or wisdom, insist we sell at favourable prices, any shrubs and plants we grow, surplus to our needs.'

'You mean undercut the nursery's prices?'

'Yes. The local nursery accused us of going into unfair competition with them. It is all to do with keeping the annual charge to residents as low as possible.'

'We understand. Mr MacMahon, could you please tell me if you've ever employed a lady with auburn or blonde hair in park work?'

'No. Never. Not to my knowledge.'

'Do you know of any architects, draughts-men or carpenters living, or with work premises in Southfield?

'Apart from Guests, the estate agents in the group of shops, no. They might draw up the occasional plan so they might boast an architect or draughtsman. Incidentally, they collect the park maintenance charge and pay our wages here. Don't upset them by linking my name with your inquiries. Please be tactful.'

'Now, where have we heard that phrase before?'

Flora turned and grinned at Essach.

The detectives visited Guests and described the carpenter's pencil stub.

'Sorry, can't help you,' said Simon Guest, 'I use an HB which I buy from the stationers next door.'

'Have you ever employed a lady with auburn or blonde hair?'

Simon Guest looked wistful as he admitted that he'd never been that fortunate.

From there they visited the nursery and introduced themselves to Ray, the manager.

'You've come about the fox pushed over the wall of Southfield Park. Just a prank. I expect old man MacMahon has been moaning to you about it.'

'We have more important matters on our minds,' replied DI Wangdula. 'We are investigating a murder.' He described the pencil stub but Ray said that they used only indelible pencils. 'What type of garden twine or string do you use, Ray?'

'Mostly green plastic tape which we staple.'

'Twine or string?'

'I'll show you.' Ray returned with waxed twine and slightly hairy green string. 'You can buy these from any hardware shop or garden centre. We sell both.'

DS Hughes asked, 'Has a lady with auburn or blonde hair ever worked here, Ray?'

'Not to my knowledge. I've only been here five years.'

'Thanks Ray. We'll be back if we need more information.'

The two detectives continued their house-to-house inquiries, stopping only to have a bar lunch at The Hunn Hotel, before continuing. They judged that, by remaining in Southfield, and having a sandwich, for their tea, the delay would allow those residents they'd missed to return home from their places of work. That evening they completed their inquiries. Their notebooks were full of negative answers. As Essach observed, 'Such is the nature of police investigations.'

8

Superintendent Salmone had relented in not allowing Essach more helpers. He had drafted two constables to assist in inquiries. An overcast day had been a relief from the direct sunshine but had been humid and sticky. It had ended with no result from enquiries at local dentists in Southfield, and throughout the rest of Baluster.

DI Wangdula went to see Superintendent Salmone. Essach explained to his thin-lipped superior the circumstantial evidence, suggesting that someone with knowledge of Southfield Park layout had interred the body there within hours of the murder.

'That person must have had a key to open the access gate lock. They'd also been careful to lock it after they'd gone.'

'To cover their tracks,' surmised Superintendent Salmone.

'For certain, sir. Only local residents are allowed a key, but the head gardener admits that all keys cannot be accounted for. As well as the lock on the gate, a night-time security chain had been cut. They'd come prepared with a bolt cutter.'

'Mm.' Superintendent Salmone nodded his head in understanding.

'DS Hughes and I have been as tactful as possible with our inquiries but it has not been easy.'

'I know, I know. You've done your best,' sighed the Super. 'Even so, I've had a telephone call from one of the residents whose house is up for sale, complaining that detectives making inquiries into a murder in Southfield are putting off prospective purchasers from viewing his house.'

'But how could he or she know that?' expostulated Essach. 'More likely the price is too high!'

'Probably,' said the Superintendent. 'Or, maybe his wife nags him and he's looking for someone to blame. The sooner this case moves on the better.'

Essach took a deep breath before pressing on with his request. 'We need to identify the victim, sir. May I please have clearance to have a computerized three-dimensional facial reconstruction made from the victim's skull?'

'That will be expensive.'

'It's the only way forward and — '

Superintendent Salmone interrupted Essach with a wave of his hand. 'All right, but get DS Hughes to shop around and negotiate the cheapest.'

'Thank you, sir.' Essach went to the door of his superior's office, opened it and, before leaving, said, 'It will have to be distributed to the media, of course. We must hope that it does not upset the residents of Southfield too much.' He quickly closed the door behind him.

DS Flora Hughes made several telephone calls before agreeing terms with Birmingham University.

'Were they the cheapest?' asked Essach.

'No. Slightly more expensive than computer facial reconstruction specialists elsewhere, but they were friendly, helpful with directions and, most importantly, can do it tomorrow.'

'The super said the cheapest.'

'With reduced travelling time and wear and tear on the car, it is, well, technically, the cheapest!'

'Huh!' Essach accepted that he had met his match. Women always had the last word. 'I leave it in your capable hands. Oh! And don't get lost in Birmingham's one-way system.' He thought he'd get the last word in.

'Don't worry. I won't get lost. I have the incentive to make enough time to enjoy shopping in The MailBox. Who knows, I might even bump into Nick Owen!'

9

Essach took Lords Wood Road, as directed, and turned left just before reaching the railway level crossing. There was a station master's stone-built house and railway station on the corner. Also, the name of the road: Pestilence Lane. No wonder Frank Morel had skirted around giving the name of the thoroughfare in which The Cottage was situated. Too late to turn back now. Trees on the left of Pestilence Lane, on the opposite side to the railway, provided a part canopy where their branches reached across the narrow lane. Slanting sunshine found its way through the leafy covering to dapple the lane. Essach drove his car so that it straddled the mossy central area of the worn tarmac surface of the lane, and gently pulled onto the wide gravel drive, to park beside a red sports car, at the front of The Cottage.

The representative from Morels, the estate agents, was standing at the open front door. He was as smartly dressed as Essach. 'I'm Timothy.' He stretched out his left hand for Essach to shake. He held his withered right hand close to his body. 'A gem of a property this, Mr, er?'

'Wangdula. The garden is neglected,' remarked Essach.

'We call it 'conservation conscious' in the trade.' Timothy smiled. 'Good for birds and insects. Anyway, with so many people unemployed, you'll easily find someone to tame it for you. Probably a foreigner.' Timothy looked at Essach Wangdula's almond eyes. 'Hm. Yes. Let me show you over the inside. Traditional hall entrance, cloaks with loo, a living room on either side and kitchen and utilities overlooking the rear garden.' Timothy led the way from room to room.

Just then a diesel passenger train rumbled along the track at the end of the rear garden.

'And upstairs are three bedrooms and bathroom. There are loos on both ground and first floors.'

Essach followed Timothy from bedroom to bedroom.

'Original features, but we are guarded in our descriptive details because they are so desirable that they might be stolen.'

'You could ask the police to keep an eye on the property for you.'

'Well, we could, but they might just drive past The Cottage to say they'd kept an eye on

47

it. But it is doubtful if they would get out of their car and take a walk around it. You must know how it is with the police these days?'

'All too well,' murmured Essach.

'A detached cottage. Secluded. Traditional accommodation. A timber garage which could be upgraded to brick-built with a small workshop if desired. Very reasonable price. Do you have a house to sell, sir?'

'No. I'm in rented accommodation.' He looked Timothy in his ordinary, round, uninteresting eyes. 'Police quarters.'

'Oh!'

'The price may seem reasonable to you but I think it is still far too high.'

'But — '

'And I would expect to pay, for cash, and no chain, a good deal less than the asking price.'

'But — '

'And then there's the trains. I would have to put up with the noise and vibration!'

'But think how useful the service could be to you, sir, with the station only about fifty metres away. Single line track. Only about eight trains a day, and fewer on Sundays. We call it the university line because it runs between Oxford and Coventry.'

'Is there a university in Coventry?'

'Yes, Mr Wangdula. Warwick University.'

'Do the trains actually stop at this station?' Essach held his head to one side in query.

'Oh yes, sir. It's a request stop. You only have to put your arm out to signal to the train driver to stop and take you on board.'

Essach smiled. 'How very quaint!'

'I think I could take a little off the price, sir.'

'For the name of the lane alone I would expect a substantial reduction. And I do mean a substantial reduction. Pestilence Lane. Hah!' As Essach left The Cottage he was interested to see how the sports car had been adapted for use by a one-armed driver.

⋆ ⋆ ⋆

Two days later Flora and Essach studied the computer image of the murder victim.

'Quite good looking,' murmured Flora.

'I wonder if he had hair, or shaved his head as a lot of young men do these days, or was balding,' mused Essach.

'Could have been a ladies' man.'

'And a jealous rival murdered him, to prevent another lady from having him?'

Flora swivelled her chair to face Essach. 'The auburn-cum-blonde hair? Hm. A possibility.'

'Well, let's encourage the media to circulate

his description and image. Once we can identify him we can scratch around for motivation and opportunity for his killing.'

* * *

During the previous day, Essach had been able to fit in a return trip to Pestilence Lane. Between The Cottage and the station house the land was cultivated. The garden land belonging to the station house, Essach surmised. Essach stopped his car and looked over the low beech hedge. It was planted with kitchen vegetables, and had a soft fruit area covered in a green mesh to keep birds out.

He then walked along to The Cottage. He could see through the wrought-iron side gate that the boundaries seemed to all consist of pyracantha or blackthorn, both providing thorny barriers for protection. On the side of The Cottage furthest from the station house, and behind a blackthorn hedge, he could make out fruit trees. Essach judged the rear garden to be about twenty metres from the back of the house to the railway boundary.

Walking along Pestilence Lane away from The Cottage, he came to a break in the hedge. It allowed him to see a caravan partly concealed from the lane. He returned to his car.

Driving his car slowly, Essach explored the narrow lane. It had vehicle passing places every so often. There was a farm on the left-hand side framed against fields. On the right-hand side was a long narrow field between the lane and the railway. On the opposite side of the railway, woodland occupied a gentle rise, and made a pleasant background. He'd noticed it rising from behind the station house and continuing behind The Cottage, and right up to here.

Pestilence Lane ended at a crossroads with a signpost pointing to local villages in leafy Warwickshire, and to Baluster, the way he had come. Doing a nifty three-point turn, he returned to Lords Wood Road. He noted that the name of the railway station was Tom Knocker's station.

Thinking, on his return to his flat, Essach considered. The railway line was probably used by trains taking commuters between Warwick and Royal Leamington Spa to and from London, travelling eastwards through Bicester, where his furniture was stored.

Sitting down in his police flat, Essach typed, Pestilence Lane, Baluster, into his laptop. The name was evidently ancient; reputed to be fourteenth-century, and so called from the pits that were dug there to bury the bodies of the victims of the Black

Death. Could have been worse, Essach thought to himself philosophically. Could have been Plague Pits Lane!

He then typed in Tom Knocker's railway station. The area had once belonged to the Knocker family. The woods on the opposite side of the railway from The Cottage were known as Lords Wood. Lord Tom Knocker had influenced the position of the railway to be built on his land in 1849. Much of his subsequent wealth had resulted from the timber cut from the woods and transported to London via the railway. His house lay behind the woods fringing the opposite side of Pestilence Lane to The Cottage, known locally as Tom Knocker's Wood.

10

A brief article, accompanied by face-on and profile photographs of the computer facial reconstruction of the murder victim, was circulated in all of the national newspapers and the *Baluster Post.*

The response was disappointing. Several telephone calls were received by Flora and Essach.

'Don't people read their newspaper?' asked Essach. 'That's the third I've had where they say they've seen the man recently in the local pub or supermarket.'

'Probably buy it for the crosswords. If they don't complete the crossword then they throw the newspaper away without bothering to read it. As I've seen you do!' Flora raised her eyebrows, daring Essach to deny it.

Of course. Flora had seen him looking in the *Baluster Post* for a suitable house, and made the wrong deduction. It was frustrating, but Essach was not about to enlighten her. 'Huh! Now what? *Crime Watch?* I'd prefer appearing on that than revisiting the residents of Southfield with photographs of the victim.'

Flora shuddered. 'I wholeheartedly agree.

I'll organize it so that we are both in the TV studio on the night,' she smiled disarmingly.

⋆ ⋆ ⋆

She read and re-read the newspaper article. Spit, stocking tops and lavatory seats, she thought, as Mother used to say. I was sure I'd buried that evil man where he'd never be found. Shocked at the reasonable likeness of the computer-generated facial reconstruction, a chill ran down her spine. Then a comforting thought took over. Even if he was identified, the police would never trace her. There was nothing to connect them. Nothing that they could ever find out. They would never find her, they would never find his murderer.

However, her thoughts continued, what about her first victim? For her peace of mind's sake, she would have to check out that her pond had not been disturbed. If his skeleton was found, then it should not be long before the police would want to talk to her.

⋆ ⋆ ⋆

Essach answered his mobile telephone, 'Hello?'

'Frank Morel here, Mr Wangdula. The

estate agent. Now, about that delightful cottage in Pestilence Lane, Timothy showed you over. An amusing name. Very historic. Goes back centuries. A talking point when you have friends around to dinner. My client is prepared to reduce the price by £1,000. What do you say to that as a generous compromise?'

'Mr Morel, yours or your client's definition of generous must have been taken from a parsimonious dictionary.'

'Eh?'

'And just whereabouts is the Black Death pit or pits in Pestilence Lane? If I want to plant a rose bush, I suppose I'm not likely to dig up a skeleton in the back garden — or am I? I get enough of those in my work.'

'Eh?'

'Ninety thousand pounds, cash, and to include your client bearing the cost of having the cesspit emptied, filling the central heating fuel tank with domestic heating oil and having a professional garden makeover.'

'Will Alan Titchmarsh do, Mr Wangdula?'

Essach ignored the sarcasm. He really wanted that house. Besides, it was the only one locally which he might be able to afford without the imposition of a mortgage.

'Just think about my offer, Mr Morel. The Cottage appears to have been on the market for quite a long time. Far too long.' Essach switched his mobile off.

* * *

Flora had made arrangements for them to stay in the same hotel in Cardiff on the night that *Crime Watch* was to be broadcast. That day soon came and they travelled by train. They admired the fields bright with sulphur-coloured rape-seed oil crops in the early July sunshine.

'Looking at the Welsh hills, the rocky outcrops, valleys and rivers, I wonder if the Tibetan scenery is similar?'

'If it is then it must be very beautiful,' replied Flora comfortingly. 'I was born in Swansea. My father is a car mechanic. We spent many happy Sundays on the Gower Coast. What about you, Essach?'

'My parents were born in Lhasa, Tibet. When the Chinese invaded they escaped with His Holiness, the Dalai Lama's party. I was born in London. Family tradition has it that my great, great grandfather, the first Essach, Sherlock Holmes — thus the initials SH, ess aitch — came from London as a consulting detective, to Tibet where he saved the life of the then Dalai Lama. He obviously had an affair with my great, great grandmother,

56

Langel Wangdula.'

When they arrived, Flora pulled a small suitcase on wheels, and Essach carried a holdall. They were allocated rooms at the hotel on the same floor close to the lift. They dined early together and then arranged to meet at 7.30 in the foyer.

Essach had showered when he arrived and so had only to clean his teeth, brush his ubiquitous charcoal-grey suit and straighten his bottle-green tie. He checked his highly polished black shoes, his miniature compass cufflinks and then sat in a comfortable chair to attempt the crossword in his newspaper. He seldom tried the crossword but it would give him the excuse to buy a national newspaper. It would also give him the reason for buying the local newspaper while he was still looking for a house. Stung by what Flora had said about people buying their newspaper just for the crossword, and not bothering to read the news, he skimmed through it quickly, just in case Flora wanted to discuss a news item she'd seen. He then returned to the crossword. He became so engrossed in solving the clues that he was startled to hear a rap on the door. He looked at his wristwatch to find that it was 7.25.

Leaving his room, Essach saw a shapely

blonde, dressed in a smart, pale blue suit with white trim, and carrying a white handbag, waiting for the lift. He heard it arrive and the blonde stepped in. He sprinted the few yards in time to enter the lift just as the doors were beginning to close.

'Good evening ... good heavens!' he exclaimed. Flora appeared to be wearing a blonde wig.

Flora smiled with an amused look on her face and crinkles formed at the sides of her pale blue eyes.

'I, er ... It is you, Flora, isn't it?'

'Sure,' Flora replied, 'it is me, myself, 'tis I. All ladies have their secrets, Essach. You've just discovered one of mine.'

Essach's nostrils caught a momentary whiff of the delicate perfume that Flora was wearing.

'My right eye is blue and my left is brown. I have twenty-twenty sight but I wear either one blue or one brown compensating contact lens. Tonight it's the blue one.'

The lift arrived at the ground floor and Essach followed Flora into the hotel foyer trying to smell her tantalizingly subtle perfume again.

Once out of the hotel, Essach walked on the outside of the pavement beside Flora.

'So the brown hair is your natural hair and

you are wearing a blonde wig now?' queried Essach.

'Ah! Another of my secrets. This is my natural hair. I wear a brunette wig and a brown contact lens for work.'

'Mm,' murmured Essach, unsure of what to say.

'Blondes have the unfortunate and unde-served reputation of being dumb. The intelligence of brunettes is hardly ever questioned. I consider that my promotion is partly attributable to my brunette persona. Would you say that I'm dumb, Essach?'

'Certainly not. I've found you to be very astute. The superintendent thinks very highly of you.'

They turned into the Cardiff BBC Broadcasting House.

★　★　★

Later, after the broadcast, in which they both appeared as being the investigating officers, Flora and Essach were passed crime informa-tion data notes taken as a result of the *Crime Watch* programme, each dated, with the time the caller made contact, and the substance of the information given. The block capitals, although hurriedly written, were easier to read than script — easier than most peoples'

59

handwriting. One stood out from all of the others. The caller was absolutely certain that the victim was an Adrian Hill, an ex-employee, who had gone missing without reason or explanation some two years ago.

11

'Essach?'

'Yes.'

'Why do you always use your own car instead of one from the pool? It could save on wear and tear on your own car.'

'Simple answer, really. Because pool cars do not have CD players.'

Essach was driving on the M40 with its wild flower swathed banks, and frequent bright yellow fields on either side.

They both lowered their sun visors.

'We'll need the sun visors just as much when we return home.'

Flora murmured agreement She sat beside him on their way to London to keep an appointment with last night's *Crime Watch* caller. She had returned to being brunette. Essach extracted a CD from a holder and inserted it into the player. The car was filled with a simple tune accompanied by a melodious voice singing 'Let's go home.'

'I've not heard that before.'

'Lok dro. Let's go home.'

'What language is that?' asked Flora.

'Tibetan. That's Techung. He plays a

piwang. A sort of violin on a drum.' The tune changed. 'Now he's singing *Snow Lion of Peace*, an independence song, a freedom song. I was born in London but my ancestors were born in Tibet, except the first Essach, my great, great grandfather. It saddens me, and all Tibetans, that our homeland is under the yoke of the Chinese barbarians.'

'Oh!'

'Men have their secrets too, Flora.'

'Ouch!'

The M40 ran into the A40.

'Do you want me to direct you, Essach? Where's your A to Z of London?'

'Thanks, Flora, but I'm on home territory. I was born in Acton and my parents had the Oriental Emporium close to Horn Lane where we're going.' Essach switched the CD of Techung off. 'Must take extra care. Lots of cyclists in Ealing, West Ealing, and Acton. I've often wondered why the local authority does not mark out cycle lanes to make using the roads hereabouts safer for motorists and cyclists alike.' He manoeuvred his car into a roadside parking space near to the estate agents.

'I can tell from your face what you are thinking, Flora. Yes, estate agents can be devious, I've dealt with some, so I do know. However, I've spoken to Mr Sullivan and he sounded very genuine to me. My parents have used the firm and so I have every confidence in him. I know, you talk to the secretaries while I talk to him. Ladies are more likely to confide in another lady than in a 'foreigner'. Believe me, I know. We'll compare notes later.'

'Yes, sir,' replied Flora sarcastically.

They entered the reception area to MRS HOMES, Estate Agents, Valuers and Surveyors.

They were ushered into Kieran Sullivan's office, where they were offered coffee. The estate agent looked at Flora with a puzzled expression on his face. Flora did not enlighten him as to why she appeared different to him today.

Introductions over, Essach considered that it would do no harm to start proceedings off with a compliment. 'I've always admired your firm's name, Mr Sullivan.'

'Ah. I'm glad you like it. It sounds a lot better than Marshall, Robinson and Sullivan. My idea. MRS HOMES is more appealing to the discerning female home seeker. I'll let you into an estate agent's secret. If you can interest the lady in a marriage or partnership in a property, she will sell it to the man in her life. The man sees in that house only gardening and decorating as a chore, the lady does not see a chore; she sees it as the way to turn that house into a home. It is she who does the final selling. In the end, the lady makes the better estate agent.' He shrugged and held his arms forward, hands turned uppermost, in gallic fashion. 'So why not begin with attracting the lady with a friendly female name like MRS HOMES?'

Flora concealed her smile.

'What can you tell us about Adrian Hill, Mr Sullivan?'

'He was a chartered surveyor who carried out survey work for clients of ours. A very good surveyor, I might add. He also used to prepare HIPS reports. A waste of clients' money, those were!'

'Mm. Yes, I think anyone with basic common sense would agree with you there. I'd want to instruct my own independent surveyor if I bought a house.'

All three sat nodding their agreement.

'I used to live around here. My parents ran the Oriental Emporium just along this road. Your firm acted on their behalf. Mr Marshall, if I remember correctly. Yes. It was he who sold their business and premises when they retired to live in India.'

'I remember now. I thought your name was familiar to me.'

'And when did Adrian Hill leave your employ?'

'A couple of years ago. Middle of June. He just failed to turn up for work. I went round to his flat. Would you believe, his landlady was clearing out his possessions. Apparently he'd decamped on the Saturday night. Taken clothing, his laptop, and his surveying tools, and left his keys in his flat door lock. There was no sign of his car. Adrian disappearing like that left us in the lurch. Had to find another surveyor fast. I never even thought that he could have been murdered. I brought his clothing, such as he'd left behind, and some personal items and put them in our storeroom in case he should return. I wrote to his mother a couple of times but I received no reply. His possessions are still in the storeroom.'

'Could your secretary provide us with Adrian Hill's mother's address, please, Mr Sullivan?' asked Flora.

The estate agent used his intercom. 'Miriam, can you find Adrian Hill's mother's address, please?'

'I'll go to Miriam,' said Flora. 'She's probably busy. And I might be able to help her sort through the relevant file.' She left the office taking her coffee cup with her.

'What can you tell me about Adrian Hill, Mr Sullivan? His habits, his dentist, his friends, girlfriends. Anything, no matter how unimportant it might seem to you, might be the lead we need to find his murderer.'

'Adrian was an MRICS, a Member of the Royal Institution of Chartered Surveyors. A very good surveyor. Nothing escaped him.'

'So you've said.'

'Always short of cash. Kept the bookmaker, three doors away, in fine wines and cigars.'

'No girlfriends?'

'I think he did have one. But an on off relationship as I understand. Miriam might be able to tell you more than I can.'

'So Adrian Hill had money troubles.'

'Yes. Could be the motive for his murder. I was shocked to see his face on *Crimewatch* last night.'

'I wonder, if I gave you a receipt for them, if I could take Adrian Hill's possessions,' said Essach. 'You never know, there might be a clue amongst them. In any case, they should be handed over to his mother, and the police can take care of that.'

'Certainly. I'll fetch them for you.'

Presently, Kieran Sullivan returned with a cardboard box, followed by three more. 'That's the lot!'

DI Wangdula handed over a receipt before he and Flora loaded them into the boot of his car.

'Adrian Hill was a gambler. Let's go and

talk to the bookie. Then we'll have some lunch.'

Flora brightened. She and Essach showed their warrant cards and were ushered into the bookmaker's office. There, they learned that Adrian Hill had backed horses, with the occasional winner, but mostly losers. He did not owe the bookmaker any money.

'No motive for the bookmaker to murder Adrian Hill, then!' Flora sighed.

'No,' said Essach dolefully. Before we go to lunch, would you mind if I took a nostalgic look at the old Oriental Emporium?'

'Not at all. Which way is it?'

Essach pointed. They walked the relatively short distance to a shop with a wide frontage. 'The buyers have kept the old name,' remarked Essach. 'Sensible. My parents built a goodwill second to none for fairness and service.'

'Do you want to go inside?' asked Flora.

'Not really. Let's just look at the Japanese water features.'

Flora noted that Essach seemed interested in that part of the rear garden which could be seen between the decorative curls in the wrought iron side gate.

'Right. Lunch, and then back to HQ. Thanks for indulging me. Something for me to write about in my next letter to my parents.'

'Something about the rear garden?'

'Well, yes. My father built a sort of mountain out of concrete in the back garden. It's gone now. The new owners must have got rid of it. When I was about nine years of age, Dad made it to put a model of the Potala Palace on it.'

Flora looked puzzled.

'The Potala Palace. His Holiness, The Dalai Lama's home in Lhasa. Dad was born in Lhasa, but he escaped with his parents soon after His Holiness escaped from Chinese rule, after they'd invaded Tibet. However, when he and Mum decided to retire, Dad put the Potala model into the box it came in, and took it with them to India.'

'It obviously left an indelible memory in your mind. Are you Bhuddist?'

'Sort of. I went to Twyford Church of England High School in Acton, and so my religious beliefs are a mixture of both Christianity and Bhuddism.' He smiled. 'It might not work for everybody, but it works for me. Enough. Lunch calls. After that, we'll get back to headquarters.'

12

Back in Baluster, Essach cleared his desk. Placing the boxes one by one onto the cleared space, he and Flora donned latex gloves before carefully removing the contents of each box. They shook out clothing and searched pockets, before carefully refolding and replacing the items in their appropriate box. Essach stacked the boxes against a wall as they finished examining the contents of each one.

Both detectives bagged items with shiny surfaces. 'I doubt whether any fingerprints found will be of any use but, who knows? His killer might have handled one or more . . . '

'I agree, Essach. Probably a dead end, no pun intended. So many seeming leads actually peter out to nothing. On the other hand, there just might be something amongst these papers. There are bank statements here.' Flora browsed through them. 'Now these will interest you.' She handed them to Essach.

After a few minutes Essach scratched his head. 'Mr Sullivan said that Adrian Hill was constantly broke, yet this bank statement puts him in funds to the tune of over £3,000.'

'Have you noticed that he paid in a grand in each of the three months, March, April and May?'

Flora and Essach looked at each other and said, in unison, 'Blackmail?'

'The bookmaker reckoned that Adrian Hill's largest win was only £200.' Essach pointed to wage slips and the corresponding amounts paid in. 'Now, that's what I call a significant break. Blackmail's as good a motive for murder as any. You can bet — ' he gave a nervous giggle ' — sorry about the pun — he probably blackmailed for double the thousand pounds. He kept back half or so, to back the horses, although we have no proof of that. But who was he blackmailing?'

'I'm not impressed with the pun. Don't give up the day job, Essach. It is most likely that his mark lives in London.'

'I think it would be tactful if we were to call on his mother first, don't you think? The super is dead keen on tact and it is our duty to tell her the sad news. I'll drop her a line to advise her when we'd like to visit.'

13

'This job certainly gets us around,' remarked Essach, setting his satnav. 'I don't know Hinckley at all.' He slipped a CD in the car player.

'Techung?' Flora asked.

'Yes. Do you mind?'

'Not at all. I quite like his music. What's he singing now?'

'*Fresh Rice Chang.*'

'Oh! Makes me hungry to even think of it. My turn to buy lunch today. I'll treat you to a Chinese.'

Essach sighed; he wasn't keen on the Chinese because they had invaded Tibet, but he did like their food.

The main shopping street in Hinckley was surprisingly steep.

'A lot of charity shops here,' remarked Flora.

'I read somewhere that it is often an indication of exorbitant shop rents locally. Charity shops are the only ones which can afford them. Lower community charge, no outlay for stock as it is all donated to them and volunteer staff. That's how they can afford sky high rents.'

'I wonder that they can sell stuff that is only fit to be given away.'

'Ah,' replied Essach, 'you haven't charity shopped in the better areas of London. Good quality shoes and suits. Do try Chelsea, Kensington and Mayfair.'

'Dead men's shoes?'

Essach gulped. 'Ah! This is it.' He stopped the car outside a modern compact detached house. Walls covered in white marble pebbledash chippings sparkled in the sunshine. 'Mrs Hill phoned to say that she will be at home.'

He rang the doorbell. They held their warrant cards at the ready.

The front door opened revealing a tall angular woman with greying hair. She wore a summer floral frock and a cardigan. 'I've been expecting you. Close the door behind you.'

They followed her into the rear lounge. The French doors were open slightly and a light breeze wafted in floral scents. She indicated for them to sit on the settee. 'Although it is a nice summer day I prefer to sit inside my home out of the rays of the sun. I hope you don't mind.'

'We're fine, Mrs Hill, thank you. I'm Detective Inspector Essach Wangdula.'

'And I'm Detective Sergeant Flora Hughes.'

'You've come about my son, Adrian.' Mrs Hill stated rather than asked.

'Well, yes,' said Essach.

'I saw his face on *Crimewatch*. Yours too.' Turning to Flora she asked, 'Weren't you the blonde?'

'I sometimes wear a wig,' Flora blurted out.

'You didn't think to contact us, Mrs Hill?'

'No. Why should I? After the way he's treated Margery and me.'

'Margery?' queried Flora.

Mrs Hill sighed. 'I'd better explain.'

Essach and Flora listened attentively while Mrs Hill told them why she was indifferent to her son's death. Margery and he had become engaged, bought a villa in the town and set up home there. 'Lived together. As young people do.' She explained that everything seemed to be all right for a time; Adrian was happy working for a local estate agency. Then he sued a local firm of chartered surveyors for negligence. He reckoned they'd missed subsidence of the rear flank wall, and he was seeking substantial damages. 'Chartered surveyors have to have professional indemnity insurance to cover them if claims are made against them. Adrian thought they'd just pay up to preserve their reputation, but they contested his claim.'

'But Adrian was a chartered surveyor himself, Mrs Hill. We've been told that he was a very good surveyor. Surely, he would not have missed such a defect?'

'No, nor did he, Mr Wangdula. It transpired that he was desperately in debt as a result of gambling. He ill-advised thought that that was his way out of financial disaster. He was unable to prove his case and consequently ended up owing even more money in solicitors' fees and compensation.'

'Who were the surveyors, Mrs Hill?'

Flora made a note of their name and address.

'Poor Margery. Didn't know what had hit her. Next thing was that Adrian had disappeared, and then the building society repossessed the house. Margery went back to her parents' home but found that she was still responsible for the negative equity, and outstanding gas and electricity bills, and community charge. You name it, it was owing. I couldn't see Margery go bankrupt, and my son,' she said, bitterly, 'had used his key to here when I was out and taken anything portable of value, so I raised money by selling what remained, and cashing in investments. Investments carefully chosen by my late husband intended to give us a comfortable retirement. I just get by now but wonder how long before I have to downsize to pay my way.'

'Oh dear,' ventured Essach, 'and there are Adrian's funeral expenses!'

⋆   ⋆   ⋆

'That wasn't very tactful, Essach. No wonder the super was worried about sending you into Southfields unaccompanied.'

'Um! Oh dear. I should have thought aloud and spoken in silence.'

'Well,' remarked Flora, 'if anyone had a motive for killing Adrian Hill . . . '

'Ah, here it is.' Essach stopped the car outside MIND in Castle Street to allow Flora to take the boxes containing Adrian Hill's clothing into the charity shop.

'I only hope that you know what you are doing, Essach. There could be clues amongst those clothes.'

'Mrs Hill doesn't want them and nor do we. Both forensics and I have been through them thoroughly. Trust me, I'm a detective.'

Flora snorted in derision.

Essach eased the car gently further down Castle Street and pulled into an off-road car park behind Grainge-Mitchell, estate agents and parked in a space marked 'Private'.

They walked around to the front and entered.

'Good day, how can I help you?' A mousy-haired middle-aged woman peered at them from behind a computer screen.

Essach held up his warrant card and Flora followed suit. 'We're here on police business. Is Mr Grainge-Mitchell in, please?'

'Just a moment.' The woman disappeared through a door behind her.

'Mrs Grainge-Mitchell will see you.'

An auburn-haired woman in her thirties emerged. 'I'm Elaine Grainge-Mitchell. How can I help you?' She waved her hand to indicate for them to follow her. 'Please do sit.'

'We're here about Adrian Hill. He's been murdered,' stated Essach.

Elaine Grainge-Mitchell's amber eyes opened wide. 'Murdered! Well, I never did like the man, but I don't see how I can 'assist you with inquiries', is what I think you say.'

'Please tell us what dealings you had with him,' said Flora gently.

Elaine Grainge-Mitchell's eyes narrowed. 'Steve, my husband and I had just opened our office here.'

'As estate agents and surveyors? I noticed that you are both chartered surveyors from your certificates on the outer office wall,' observed Essach.

'Adrian Hill came in here, all 'Elaine and Steve, and I'm Adrian', as though we'd known him for years. He told us that he'd agreed to buy a house and needed to get in quickly. He said that, as a fellow chartered surveyor, his inspection revealed no problems. He'd recommended us to his building society and they'd added our name to their list of surveyors.'

'Very nice of him, surely?' Flora cocked her head.

'The only good thing he did. We still get work from them. Anyway, Steve did the survey and the only remark he included was that, 'the borrower should get the drains tested'. We heard no more until the building society said that he'd made a complaint against us and was seeking compensation of £25,000. He said that the flank wall had bulged. Steve and I went to inspect the flank wall together. That wall had been re-pointed before Steve inspected and hadn't moved since his survey. We asked Adrian Hill if he'd had the drains tested, which he should have done as a condition of his mortgage loan. He admitted that he hadn't. We reported back to the building society and promptly sued Adrian Hill for malicious accusations. We settled out of court and it cost Adrian Hill a considerable sum of money. He paid up in order to keep his qualification. And that's what our dealings with Adrian Hill were,' she ended, bitterly.

'What an evil thing for one chartered surveyor to do to another!' remarked Flora.

'Mrs Grainge-Mitchell, would you be able to advise us of your whereabouts on the 17 June two years ago?'

The lady surveyor looked at Essach curiously before taking a diary out of a bookcase. She turned pages. 'Yes, Steve and I were in London that weekend. We went to see *Phantom of the Opera*.'

Essach and Flora waited until Steve Grainge-Mitchell arrived as a matter of courtesy before setting off to find a Chinese restaurant.

After their meal they set off to call on Margery. When they called at Margery's parents' home, Flora gently explained to them the purpose of their visit.

'As if the poor girl hasn't had enough to put up with!' exclaimed Mrs Hollingworth. 'If looks could have killed! Well then, but my daughter is no murderer.'

'It is something we have to do, Mrs Hollingworth. Interview Margery.'

'I hope you don't catch him, the murderer. He's done society a great service.'

Margery was a honey-blonde and only five feet three inches tall. She had nothing new to tell them except that she'd met someone else and never wanted to hear Adrian Hill's name again.

14

'Well, we have one possible suspect. And she had the motive and opportunity.' Essach and Flora sat at Essach's desk.

'But Elaine Grainge-Mitchell had had her revenge. She's not really a prime suspect,' observed Flora. 'And I can't see Margery as a killer, can you? She's too timid and hardly strong enough to manually strangle anything larger than a spider.'

'And she does not have the right colour hair!'

'Shame about the estate agents. They could well be capable. Two people working together to bury the body makes perfect sense. But how would they have had access to a key to the park? We must ask around Southfield and see if anyone remembers them carrying out work in that area,' said Essach. 'Just in case. That does bother me. The person or persons we are looking for have had to have lived or worked in Southfield, or both, to know about the private park. And they must somehow have obtained a key. Our murderer must have been resident in Baluster at some time. Might still live here, even . . . '

'Or, a former resident who now lives in London,' Flora finished what Essach was thinking. 'Another visit to MRS HOMES is called for. There must be something we've missed. Maybe we didn't ask the right questions.'

★ ★ ★

'Frank Morel here, Mr Wangdula. I've discussed your circumstances with the vendors and your ability to complete the purchase of The Cottage quite quickly. If you would care to consider paying something in excess of £90,000 I'm sure that we can come to an agreement.'

'Oh dear!'

'The septic tank is empty and I have the receipt.'

'Um.'

'And I have the HIPS report.'

'If I agree to purchase I'll have my own survey carried out, thank you very much, Mr Morel.'

'May I please receive your offer in writing, Mr Wangdula? Your solicitor will help you. Put in, 'subject to satisfactory survey and searches', if you write the letter yourself.'

Essach wondered whether to mention the state of the garden, but then remembered Mr

Morel's previous sarcastic remark, and thought better of it.

'In excess of £90,000, you say? I'll think about it and put my offer in writing.'

* * *

'Sorry to trouble you again, Mr Sullivan,' Essach apologized into the telephone receiver, 'but we are still looking for clues which will lead us to the breakthrough which will enable us to find Adrian Hill's killer.'

'What else can I tell you, Detective Inspector?'

'Can you remember anything unusual that happened involving Adrian Hill while he was with you? Anything. No matter how small and insignificant it may seem to you, it might turn out to be important to us. What you've given us has already suggested a possible motive for his murder.' Anticipating Kieran Sullivan's next question, Essach continued, 'I'm afraid that I am not in a position to divulge what that is, Mr Sullivan.'

'Ah! I do understand. But I don't think that I can help you any more than I have. You didn't find anything of significance in his possessions which we gave you?'

'We did, but as I said, I am not at liberty to reveal what that is. Do you know if Adrian

Hill recently came into money?'

Kieran Sullivan replied, 'Well no. Not to my knowledge. But now I come to think of it, he didn't ask for a sub during the last few weeks before he disappeared.'

'Mm. That figures.'

Flora said, 'Ask him, does he mind if we talk to the lady who works part-time in the front office, and who wasn't there when we called.'

Essach frowned.

'Something I found out from Miriam.'

Essach put the question to Kieran Sullivan.

'By all means. She'll be here tomorrow afternoon. We have to employ part-time staff. The public expects estate agents to be available seven days a week, but our staff mainly work a five day week, so part time staff take over for them to have their two days off. Also, the partners try to take two Saturdays and Sundays out of every three to be with our families. One partner must be available while the two others are relaxing.'

'We here in the police know the feeling well, Mr Sullivan.'

'Right then, I'll tell Mrs Cooper to expect you.'

15

Closing her umbrella, Flora entered the reception area of MRS HOMES estate agents, closely followed by Essach. A lady sat behind a computer screen. She was dressed in a black skirt and crisp white blouse with a floppy black bow tie at the throat. Streaks of grey contrasted with her jet black hair. The friendly smile she gave them crinkled the skin at the sides of her grey eyes. 'I'm Margaret Cooper. I was expecting you.'

The two detectives introduced themselves.

'Excuse me one moment.' Mrs Cooper pressed 'print' on the computer and a printer in the corner of the office sprang into action. She rose and shook hands with them. 'How can I help you?'

Flora explained that because Adrian had disappeared while in London that the police believed he'd been murdered here, even though his skeleton had been found in Baluster. It followed, therefore, that his murderer, or murderers could have been in contact with him, here, in London. Did any event spring to mind? Something out of the ordinary?

Just then Kieran Sullivan opened the door, shook his umbrella, came in out of the rain and wiped his shoes on the coco-fibre doormat.

'Hm. Let me think.' Mrs Cooper crossed to the printer to satisfy herself that all was in order. 'Adrian and I were the only ones here one day. A very tall blonde lady came into the office and asked for him. He must have recognized her voice because he came straight out of the side office he used to use. He took her in there and an almighty row took place. It was something to do with a survey he carried out at a property in Friendship Road.'

Kieran Sullivan took a handkerchief out of a pocket and wiped rain from his face. 'The rain is almost horizontal out there.'

Neither woman responded. Essach merely nodded.

'Could you hear what was said, Margaret?' asked Flora.

'Not really. I think I heard that she wanted something, but I don't know what.'

'I heard the property in Friendship Road mentioned. Sorry to interrupt,' interjected Kieran Sullivan. 'A survey Adrian carried out. A survey not up to his usual standard. But equally memorable because the property became the subject of a rumour. Rumour only, but local gossip suggested a scandal.

However, I really don't know what it was all about.' The telephone rang. 'I'll get that. I'll take it in my office. I'm expecting a call from Martin Marshall, my partner.'

'Do you know Adrian's girlfriend's name, Margaret?' asked Flora.

'Sorry. I don't think I can help you any more. Would you mind if I got on with my work, now, please?'

Essach and Flora sat in chairs comfortably upholstered for clients' and prospective purchasers' use, and waited for Kieran Sullivan to finish his telephone conversation.

Presently, the estate agent returned. 'Martin is sending round the file on 25 Friendship Road. He remembers that our replacement surveyor, who now works from our Northfields office, found something odd when he browsed through Adrian's old files, soon after joining the firm. Please, come into my office and wait for it. It'll be only about ten minutes or so.'

Essach longed to ask the estate agent for confirmation that he was going about negotiating for the cottage in Pestilence Lane in the right way. Instead, he drank the tea which Mrs Cooper had made for them. They heard someone come into the reception area.

'Ah! That'll be it.' The estate agent left his office to return with a pocket file. He wiped the raindrops off it with the sleeve of his jacket before placing the file on the desk in front of Essach; obviously being a detective inspector commanded the estate agent's respect. 'Martin Marshall says please feel free to read the survey and background notes. Oh, and by the way, look inside the file for items which are a puzzle to us.'

Essach and Flora sat side by side as they perused the survey. 25 Friendship Road, Ealing, was a six-bedroom detached residence which had been sold for a seven-figure sum. A set of details prepared by the selling agents with photographs and floor plans gave a good description. The survey report seemed to be straightforward.

Flora removed a clear plastic sandwich bag from the file. It was sealed with a staple. She smoothed the plastic and gasped when she saw the contents.

'What is it?' asked Essach.

'A two-inch nail tied to a length of garden twine.'

'Does it look as though it could be the same as the . . . ?'

'It is green and brown in parts, but yes, it looks very much the same.'

Kieran Sullivan frowned at the cryptic conversation.

'Better not open it. Let forensics do that,'

commented Essach.

'That sounds significant,' remarked the estate agent.

'It is, but I'm sure that you will understand that we are unable to discuss it while a murder investigation is ongoing.' Essach explored the folder and brought out a photograph.

'I know what that is,' volunteered the estate agent. 'See there! That's a hole in the newel post at the head of the first floor stairs. When the purchasers were having the house redecorated the painters pointed it out to them. The buyers accused Adrian of negligence in not reporting it. Of course Adrian had disappeared by then. We shelled out £200 to have it treated by a specialist firm. What we shall never understand is why, when Adrian Hill took the trouble to photograph the hole, he then neglected to include it in his report!'

'Mr Sullivan, may we take this file, complete, with us, please? I believe that it contains important information which will assist us with our inquiries to find Adrian Hill's killer.'

16

Essach and Flora sat side by side at Essach's desk. Police activity was taking place all through the open-plan office but Flora and Essach's wholehearted attention filtered out sounds and movement all around them.

The forensic report on the desk confirmed what they'd hoped for. The twine tied to the nail was identical in manufacture to the ligature found around Adrian Hill's neck, but neither of the two ends matched up with the ends of the ligature.

'What is puzzling is why part of the twine should have been coloured shades of brown,' remarked Flora. Her brown eyes searched Essach's as if seeking some explanation in his almond eyes. 'And, where did the wood particles on the twine come from?'

'There's something we're missing here. We need more information.' Essach took the sales details out of the file and placed them on his desk. They'd been prepared by Yeabalts, the estate agents, who sold 25 Friendship Road. 'I'll telephone Yeabalts. See what information they may hold in their files.'

The receptionist put Essach through to a

Mr Fisher. 'Lloyd Fisher here. How may I help you, Detective Inspector?'

Essach explained that he was investigating the murder of chartered surveyor, Adrian Hill, who had surveyed 25 Friendship Road, for the purchaser's mortgage company. 'Can you remember anything about this sale, Mr Fisher?'

'Very much so, Mr Wangdula. It was eventful, to say the least. The house came on to the market because the owner, Mr Swindell-Banks, had been killed accidentally falling down the stairs. He was elderly. In his mid sixties as I understand it.'

Is mid sixties elderly? wondered Essach.

'Was there an inquest, Mr Fisher? Can you remember?'

'Oh yes. The verdict was accidental death.'

'Oh!'

'You sound surprised, Mr Wangdula.'

'Mm.'

'You have heard rumours about a family scandal, I suppose?'

Essach Wangdula's ears pricked up. He indicated for Flora to pick up a nearby phone and listen in as far as possible. 'Please go on about the scandal rumour, Mr Fisher.'

'Apparently Mr Swindell-Banks had assigned half ownership in the house to his house-keeper. There was talk of it going to court, but in the end, the family decided to share the proceeds with ... hm ... can't think of her name at the moment, but it will come to me. Just a moment while I ask for the relevant files to be brought to me.'

Essach and Flora heard noises in the background.

'Are you still there?'

Essach grunted assent.

'Ah. Where was I? Oh, yes. The family were afraid of publicity, as I understand it, some sort of embarrassing scandal. Apparently, they would rather cover it up, than fight the housekeeper in court for over £1 million. Some scandal, eh?'

'Do you know, Mr Fisher, if the housekeeper was in 25 Friendship Road, when Mr Swindell-Banks fell down the stairs?'

'No. As I understand it, he was in the house alone. His housekeeper had forgotten her keys when she went shopping. When she returned she rang the doorbell and knocked so loudly that she disturbed the neighbours. Apparently, Mr Swindell-Banks had taken a sleeping pill and his housekeeper could not rouse him. However, she made such a racket that someone, a neighbour, I suppose, called the police, and Mr Swindell-Banks's son. Anyway, as I understand it, young Mr Swindell-Banks was just about to use his key to let them in when they heard the old man cry out as he fell down the stairs. Half asleep, I suppose.'

'Just a moment, Mr Fisher, while I confer with my colleague.'

'What's on your mind, Essach?' inquired Flora.

'I was thinking that Mr Swindell-Banks might have tripped on a certain piece of twine. A tripwire, so to speak. Just a moment, please.'

Before he could speak, Lloyd Fisher's voice came over the telephone, 'Mr Wangdula, I now have our files.'

'Mr Fisher, do you, by any chance, have a video of 25 Friendship Road, which you might have used for internet advertising, please?'

'Certainly. Computer memory is so vast these days that we never erase anything. Please give me your email address and I'll have it sent as an attachment.'

Essach gave Lloyd Fisher the address and asked the estate agent to keep the file handy as he would be grateful for further information. He explained to Flora, that if they could establish that the twine had been used as a tripwire, it ought to be possible to work out why and how it had been found by Adrian Hill and had been missed by the police. 'Ah! There's Yeabalt's email, if I'm not mistaken.'

Essach played the estate agents' advertisement video viewing of 25 Friendship Road. He was particularly interested when the camera panned the landing showing the position of the first floor bedrooms and family bathroom. 'There!' He pointed.

'What?'

'The skirting opposite the post at the top of the staircase.'

'The newel post. What about it?'

'It has an open joint in the skirting at the top of the stairs.'

'So, Essach? What's the significance?'

'If, and at this stage I can only conjecture, the newel post is hollow, or has been hollowed out, perhaps that supposed woodworm hole found by the decorators was actually drilled to connect with the hollow.' Essach sorted through the file on loan to him by Kieran Sullivan of MRS HOMES, the surveying firm. 'That crucial fact; evidence to you and me, was deliberately not included in Adrian Hill's survey report. Because his experience told him that that hole had been drilled deliberately to connect with the hollow in the newel post. One end of the twine could have been threaded through the supposed woodworm hole and into the hollowed newel post with the nail weighting it taut.'

'Uh, uh.'

'And the other end threaded through that open joint in the skirting opposite. Perhaps nailed. Or no, with another nail weighting it. The tripwire could have been broken by Mr Swindell-Banks as he fell.'

'And both ends would have been pulled out of sight,' Flora finished the sentence for Essach.

'Exactly!'

They both sat silently considering Essach's theory.

Flora played the video-viewing through again. The camera panning the hall clearly showed the length of the newel post. 'Is it possible to drill down the inside of that length of newel post? First of all you'd have to remove that acorn shaped knob at the bottom. I bet that's firmly glued for a start. And then you'd have to find a drill long enough to reach up to where the hole is at the head of the stairs.'

'Yes, yes,' said Essach irritably, 'but the housekeeper must have found some way of drilling it. But the question still remains, how did Adrian Hill find it, and how did he recognize its significance?'

Flora sat back in her chair. 'It certainly

could be how the housekeeper, and young Mr Swindell-Banks, and the police, were able to be outside the house when Mr Banks fell. The perfect alibi. And it explains the wood dust on the twine.'

'When over £1 million is the motive, the means of murder has to be very clever. And, if I'm right in this case, it is very clever. What we need is proof. I'd say we have evidence enough but you know our legal system. Any barrister worth his fee will plead to a sympathetic jury that what we have is merely speculative, circumstantial evidence. We still need absolute proof. A transcript of the inquest should help. Police were on hand when it happened. Who knows what else happened but was not necessary for the coroner to know? It is often the details which give us the breakthrough we need.'

'I'll organize a copy of the inquest. At long last, I get the feeling that we are getting somewhere with this investigation.'

17

Several days later, Lloyd Fisher welcomed Essach and Flora into his spacious and cool office, at Yeabalts, a contrast to the glaring sun and hot pavements of London, outside.

'How nice to meet you. We don't often come into contact with the police in our profession.' Lloyd Fisher's paternal smile added to the immediate impression of a portly fatherly figure. He indicated the detectives to be seated in soft padded chairs.

Essach looked around at the walls panelled in a pale wood with oil paintings hanging on them. Two chandeliers sparkled as he moved his head. A highly polished mahogany desk indented the Chinese carpet on which it stood.

A secretary, slim and wearing a cream coloured suit with navy-blue piping, had quietly followed them into the office. She set a tray down on a side table. 'Can I offer you tea?' she asked.

As they sipped from bone china cups, Lloyd Fisher inquired, 'Did you find the video viewing helpful, Detective Inspector?'

'Very,' responded Essach. 'Do you remember anything about the sale of 25 Friendship

96

Road, Mr Fisher?'

'Oh yes. We, Yeabalts, that is, were instructed to offer 25 Friendship Road for sale on behalf of the executor and beneficiaries of the late Mr Israel Swindell-Banks and a Mrs Ruby Stone. I'll explain. Mrs Stone was the late Mr Swindell-Banks's housekeeper and was entitled to a half-share of the proceeds of the sale of the house.' He paused, 'Mrs Stone was joint owner and was not left her share as a beneficiary of Mr Swindell-Banks's will.' Again, he paused to allow this information to sink in.

'Isn't that unusual, Mr Fisher?'

'It is indeed very unusual, Detective Inspector. And, in normal circumstance, would surely be disputed.'

'Isn't that what happened in this case, then?'

'No. The family neither disputed the sale, nor would they allow Mrs Stone access to the house again. She'd left her keys in the house when she went shopping and young Mr Swindell-Banks held on to them. We were given strict instructions, by Mr Swindell-Banks junior, that Mrs Stone was not to be given keys or to be allowed into the house — under any circumstances.'

'But surely Mrs Stone, as joint owner, was entitled — '

Lloyd Fisher interrupted Essach, 'Despite the verdict of the coroner determining that old Mr Swindell-Banks had met his death accidentally, young Mr Swindell-Banks maintained that, in his opinion, his father's death was suspicious. He even insisted that the police restrain Mrs Stone from entering 25 Friendship Road on the day that the accident happened.'

'Was there any doubt that it could have been something other than an accident, Mr Fisher?'

'No doubt whatsoever. Mrs Stone had returned from shopping to find that she'd left her keys inside. She made such a racket trying to wake old Mr Swindell-Banks who had, apparently, taken a sleeping pill the night before, that neighbours called the police, who, in turn, insisted on calling his son. They were all standing on the front doorstep, so to speak, when they heard a yell from inside the house. Young Mr Swindell-Banks said to the police, 'Hold her there. Don't let her come inside,' meaning Mrs Stone, of course. While a policewoman kept her outside, he and a policeman entered to find old Mr Swindell-Banks at the foot of the stairs. An ambulance was sent for, but he was pronounced dead. Quite a tale, don't you think, Detective Inspector?'

'What about Mrs Stone's belongings?' asked Flora.

'Young Mr Swindell-Banks packed all of her possessions into suitcases and sent her on her way. We heard all of this from his solicitor when we were instructed to sell the house.'

'I noticed that the house was devoid of any furnishings in your video. Was anything found which could be regarded as unusual when the house was being emptied, do you know?'

'No, Detective Inspector. There had been a whopping bonfire in the back garden. We instructed a firm we use from time to time, to tidy up. They buried the ashes and dug the soil over to leave the area ready for planting.'

'Well,' said Essach, 'that might be useful information. Thanks.'

'Ah, but that's not all, Detective Inspector.' The estate agent tapped the side of his nose with his forefinger. 'This is the interesting bit which, we gleaned from the mortgage surveyor, Adrian Hill and the police. It seems that when Adrian Hill was in the middle of surveying 25 Friendship Road, someone insistently rang the front doorbell. He told us that he usually ignored people calling at the property during his surveys. As he said, 'They are usually only carrying out a survey of their own, as to what products householders use, or which TV programmes they habitually watch.' When he opened the front door a tall blonde woman tried to push past him. He was too quick for her and grabbed her arm and forced it up her back. Adrian Hill threw her out. He had been warned by us not to let Mrs Stone into the house, and rightly presumed that was her. A surveyor missing an opportunity to get to know a blonde? Well, well. What is the world coming to! Eh?' Lloyd Fisher cocked his head.

The two detectives could hardly conceal their smiles at the comical picture conjured up in their minds.

'Apparently, the next thing to happen, was loud knocking on the front door. Adrian Hill opened it to, by coincidence, it later transpired, the same patrol car police who had attended when Mr Swindell-Israel Banks had fallen down the stairs.'

'I expect Friendship Road was on their beat, Mr Fisher,' commented Flora.

'Um. I expect so. Anyway, the police said that they'd had a mobile phone call from a lady at 25 Friendship Road saying that she'd been molested by a surveyor.'

'A serious accusation,' observed Flora.

'Quite so. Apparently her blouse was torn and her hair was in disarray. She demanded that the police charge Adrian Hill with assault. Anyway, to cut a long story short, something happened. I don't know what, but whatever it was, Mrs Stone changed her mind. She didn't press charges and she left the property quietly.'

'You've been most helpful, Mr Fisher. I wonder if you could let me have Mrs Stone's home address, please?'

'Everything was done through her solicitors, Detective Inspector. I'll give you their name and address.'

18

Essach and Flora found a light and airy café where they ordered sandwiches and a pot of tea for their lunch.

'Why did Ruby Stone go back to the house? What was it that was so important to her?' ruminated Flora aloud.

'It surely must have been the twine that Adrian Hill left in the survey file.' Essach scratched his head. 'But how did it come to light, I wonder?'

Just then their food was served. 'Aren't you going to pour the tea?' asked Flora.

'Yes. I'll show you the Tibetan tea ceremony. It's a bit long-winded.'

Before Essach could move, Flora had poured milk into the teacups and added tea. She had a thought, 'You've done that before!'

'When Rowena was alive.' Essach looked shamefaced.

'You wound her up,' Flora accused. 'Well, you won't wind me up.'

'The police in the patrol car,' said Essach, quickly changing the subject.

'You think they might know something useful to us?'

'It's worth a try. So far, we have the motive of money, and opportunity, resulting in a very clever murder. And we have a prime suspect.'

'But insufficient proof to convict the murderer.'

'As you say, Flora. We are fairly certain that we know how it was done but we lack proof.'

When they had finished their lunch, they called at Ealing police station, and inquired about the patrol car and police officers on the Friendship Road beat. They accepted the offer of coffee while they waited for the duty officer to put out a call for the police officers to return to the station.

'I've put WPC Crow and PC Brown in an interview room. As your inquiries relate to a murder you can tape the interview if you wish,' suggested the duty officer. 'You are fortunate that they are still together. It is because they have the appropriate tact and elocution needed for the upmarket residential area of Ealing.'

The two constables stood as Flora and Essach entered the interview room.

'Please relax,' said Essach, 'you are not in any trouble, but we do need all the help that you can give us.' He introduced themselves. 'DS Hughes, and I am DI Wangdula.' He noticed WPC Crow's reaction at seeing him.

'I can see that you remember me from somewhere.'

'We were both at Brent Station at the same time, sir,' she replied, in a well modulated voice.

'Can you cast your minds back two years? You were directed to domestic incidents at 25 Friendship Road on two occasions.' Essach could see from their faces that they did remember. 'Good. We have enough information on your first call: Mr Swindell-Banks senior fell down the stairs while you were outside the house; Mr Swindell-Banks junior insisted that you kept the housekeeper, a Mrs Ruby Stone, from entering the house.'

'Yes, sir,' confirmed PC Brown.

'It is the second occasion that we are interested in. Can you tell us what you can remember of what happened that time, please?'

'Mm.' PC Brown considered his beautifully articulated words. 'We were directed there to investigate a domestic incident. When we arrived, the big blonde woman, who had been denied access to 25 Friendship Road on the previous occasion, was standing on the doorstep, yet again. She said that the building society surveyor had assaulted her.'

'Her blouse was torn and her hair was a mess,' added WPC Crow.

'We knocked on the door until it was answered by the surveyor. A man. My, what a performance!'

'Adrian Hill.'

'Yes. Now that you mention it. I do remember his name.'

'Why did you say, 'What a performance,' Constable Brown?'

'Because the blonde woman should have been an actress. She towered above all three of us. And she was well built.'

'Statuesque,' added WPC Crow.

'Yet she would have had us believe that she'd been attacked by Adrian Hill.'

'The man, on the other hand,' continued Constable Brown, 'was dressed neatly with no damage to his clothing, which he must surely have suffered in assaulting such a tall and well-made woman,' he observed. 'Anyway, it was our duty to ask him what had happened and, as we did so, the woman slipped past the surveyor and into the hall. The man was not at all happy with the turn of events. He tried to explain to us that he had neither assaulted the woman nor was she supposed to be allowed access to the house.'

'While my colleague was questioning the surveyor I kept my eye on the woman,' explained WPC Crow. 'I saw her go about halfway up the stairs and reach through the banisters. Then she pulled the knob off the bottom of the newel post. I heard a metallic sound. I immediately entered the hall. I asked her what she thought she was doing.'

'By that time the surveyor had convinced me that the woman should not be in the house and that her claim of assault was merely a ruse to help her get in there,' said PC Brown. 'I quickly joined WPC Crow and, not without difficulty, we bundled her out of the house. She made a song and a dance at us assaulting her, and the surveyor assaulting her, and if we did not allow her into the house she would sue all of us.'

'I see what you mean by performance,' said Essach.

'But, suddenly, she stopped. She then said that she would not be bringing charges against any of us. Before we could even think to charge her with wasting police time she was off. Drove her car across the front lawn, past our vehicle, and she was away. We never saw her again.'

'Can you remember which way Mrs Stone was facing when she suddenly changed her mind?' asked Flora. 'And where was the surveyor?'

WPC Crow turned to her colleague, 'We were standing in the front doorway facing the front drive. Keeping Mrs Stone from re-entering. The surveyor was behind us in the hall.'

PC Brown agreed.

'Ah! That is what we needed to know. Thank you. Now, if both of you could create a photofit of the blonde, we'd be most grateful.' Essach ended the interview.

When the two patrol car officers had left the room, Essach heaved a sigh of satisfaction. 'That's how Adrian Hill came into possession of the twine and nail. He must have either seen it on the hall floor beneath the newel post, or heard it drop, when he was talking to the police. No, I know. The knob was missing from the bottom of the newel post. He probably dangled the nail on the twine behind the constables' backs where they couldn't see it but she could. No wonder Mrs Stone was stopped in her tracks.'

★ ★ ★

'You obviously never worked with the DI when you were at Brent station,' stated PC Brown.

'No. He had a reputation of going off the rails from time to time. A loose cannon. But I give him this, he was really successful at solving even the most difficult of murders. A proper Sherlock Holmes. He asked for a transfer when his wife died.'

*　*　*

'Motive,' remarked Essach, 'That is what bothers me. Ruby Stone's motive to kill was obviously the money she received from the sale of 25 Friendship Road. But what was the motive which induced Mr Swindell-Banks senior to sign over half of the ownership of his valuable home?'

'Some form of blackmail, do you think?' asked Flora.

'No. Not blackmail. People don't live in the same house as their blackmailer. No, there has to be another motive.'

'Sex.'

Essach turned his head sharply. 'Sex! I know that it is a strong motive, but a man as rich as Israel Swindell-Banks was could have afforded to pay a high-class call girl. Surely not sex!'

'But Lloyd Fisher said that the family wouldn't sue because of a scandal. What if it was a scandal connected with sex — but much worse than just ordinary sex?' suggested Flora.

'Worse than just ordinary sex? I, for one, do not want to go there. You mean something scandalous which, if it had come out in court proceedings, would have brought down shame and dishonour on the family? Ah, yes, now you are talking motive. A strong motive. Mm. Which of course, it has to be, a very strong motive, indeed. What exactly was it that induced Mr Swindell-Banks to make over a half-share of his home to his housekeeper? She must have been either a superb housekeeper, or had other attractions!' mused Essach.

'We need to talk to the family of Mr Swindell-Banks about that. We also need the other end of the twine. Let's hope that it is still behind the skirting board of 25 Friendship Road. We must find it if it is still there. That will be our proof of the so called 'perfect murder',' insisted Flora.

19

Essach explained to Superintendent Salmone how, so far, he and Flora had succeeded in solving how the murder of Mr Swindell-Banks had been achieved, despite the coroner deciding that it was an accidental death. And how the twine was a link to the murder of Adrian Hill. 'We have a prime suspect but we do not have proof. Circumstantial evidence, yes, but we need proof. Otherwise our prime suspect will get clean away. Might even go on to commit more murders. I need your clearance with the Metropolitan Police to operate in their area; to obtain the permission from the new owners of 25 Friendship Road, to obtain the other end of the twine used as a tripwire. If it is still there. If necessary, I shall need a court order.'

'I suppose so,' replied Superintendent Salmone. 'I've just thought. You mean to say that you've been making inquiries on another force's patch without seeking permission first?'

'I used to work and live in that area, sir. I guarantee that you will receive permission as long as you accept full responsibility for my actions.' Essach shook his head sadly. 'I almost think they'd gloat if I were to fail.'

'I've had my misgivings as to why a detective with your excellent record of murder detection should have been allowed a transfer.'

'The death of my wife, Rowena, sir. I wanted to restart my life in a new area. I'm beginning to relax here. Get back to my old self.'

'Ah, I'm sorry to bring back sad memories.'

Essach was noncommital. 'Without searching for proof we could be accused of negligence in our duty to bring a — '

'Yes, yes. I know all that,' said Superintendent Salmone irritably. 'I don't need lessons from you on how to do my job.'

'Yes, sir.'

'I'll get clearance from the Met. The sooner you can wind up this case the better.'

20

'While we are waiting for authority from the Met to operate on their patch, what say we re-visit Southfield?' suggested Flora. 'Our prime suspect in London is a housekeeper. I've been looking back through my house-to-house inquiries notes when Adrian Hill's skeleton was found. I interviewed a couple who were interested in the police finding their late aunt's housekeeper. They reckoned she'd stolen £350,000 from their aunt.'

Essach frowned.

'I know what you are thinking — don't upset the residents. Tact. I know that the super is not over-pleased with your request to the Met. Just the one visit. It would be interesting to find out more from that couple. For some reason I did note that they'd not been living in the house at the time when the theft took place. That couple subsequently sold their own home in the hope of finding the money still on the premises. Up to the time of my visit they'd had no success. Their aunt's housekeeper would have been ideally situated to know about Southfield private park. What if she'd obtained a key to the gate and taken it with her?'

'It would certainly link the two murders. Good idea. However, don't let Superintendent Salmone know. We'll take the photofit which Crow and Brown put together for us.'

They travelled in Essach's car to the music and voice of Techung. When they arrived at the house in Repton Drive the couple were at home.

'Mr and Mrs Wilson,' Flora asked, 'do you remember me? Detective Sergeant Hughes. This is Detective Inspector Wangdula. We've come to discuss the events surrounding your aunt's death and the alleged theft of a large sum of money. Alleged to have been taken by your aunt's housekeeper.'

'Three hundred and fifty thousand pounds,' growled Mr Wilson. 'Because I reported the theft to you lot and signed a statement to that effect, I had to pay death duty on it. We sold our own house and moved here to raise the money.'

'Now, now, Donald. The detectives have come here to be helpful. Just consider. You now have two detectives who actually want to hear what happened.'

Mrs Wilson turned to Essach and Flora, 'The police were no help at all. I'll go and make coffee. I'm sure you'd both like to join us. We usually have coffee at about this time each morning.'

'I apologize for being rude to you.'

'Don't worry about it, Mr Wilson. We, the police, that is, do not always get things right,' reassured Essach.

They talked about the weather and the state of the garden, which they could see through the lounge French window, and then the beautiful marble fireplace and over mantel mirror with its Victorian whatnot shelves, until Mrs Wilson's return with a silver coffee pot and porcelain cups and saucers.

'Before we get you to go through what happened, I suppose you wouldn't happen to have a photograph of your aunt's house-keeper?' Essach waited hopefully.

'Sorry, we don't,' replied Mrs Wilson. 'If Aunt had any they are not here now.'

'Would you care to look at the photofit we have with us here,' said Essach, placing it in front of Mrs Wilson.

Donald Wilson twisted his body so that he could see the photofit. 'That's her,' he shouted. 'That's bloody her!'

'Donald!' exploded Mrs Wilson, 'Such language! And getting excited will do your heart no good at all. Remember Aunt Lilian. She had a weak heart.'

'By 'her', who do you mean, sir?' asked Flora quietly.

'Rachael Smith. That's Rachael Smith, my late Aunt Lilian's housekeeper.'

The two detectives looked at each other, eyebrows raised.

'Would you describe her to us please, Mrs Wilson?' requested Essach.

Mr Wilson got out of his chair and went across to a bureau on the left side of the French window.

'She is very tall.'

'Six feet tall?' Essach prompted.

'No. Taller than that. Six feet three or four inches tall. She is a giantess.'

'Mm. Carry on, Mrs Wilson.'

'She has a head of lovely auburn hair; she is well rounded and strong with it. A good worker.'

'Did this Rachael Smith carry a pencil on her person, do you remember, Mrs Wilson?' asked Flora.

'Yes. Now you come to mention it. She carried a pencil stub behind her ear but it was always hidden by her hair. She said she carried it as a tribute to her father. From that we assumed that he was dead and that the pencil had once belonged to him. She must have loved him very much.'

'I think you'll be interested in this.' Mr

Wilson held out a sheet of paper.

Essach gave a low whistle. 'A reference.'

'I obtained this reference,' said Donald Wilson bitterly. 'Worst day's work I ever did. She stole — '

'Yes, yes, Donald. You've already told the detectives how much, and that you had to pay death duties on it, and that we moved here in consequence.' Mrs Wilson turned to the two detectives: 'What my husband should be telling you is, that Rachael Smith ransacked this house and took every photograph in which she appeared away with her. However, my husband kept this reference at our home of that time. Rachael Smith, I'm sure, would have taken that too if she could have found it. We showed it to the police when we reported the crime but they returned it saying that the building firm had gone out of business.'

Flora read the reference. 'Apparently, Mrs Rachael Smith was housekeeper to a Mr Joseph Peat who ran a building firm. A glowing reference. Did you contact Mr Peat, Mr Wilson?'

'I spoke to a woman, yes. After the event,' he added bitterly, 'But she was rather short with me. Said that she was the new owner of the property, and that Mr Peat didn't live there any more.'

'She didn't give a forwarding address for Mr Peat?'

'I didn't like to ask any more questions. I was too upset.'

'Naturally,' hurriedly murmured Essach before Mr Wilson could voice his complaint about being robbed. 'We'll take this with us, if we may?'

'Just a moment — I'll get you to sign a receipt.' Mr Wilson moved to the bureau to get a pen and paper.

'Can I show you something, my dear?' asked Mrs Wilson. 'Come with me. It only upsets my husband to talk about it.' Mrs Wilson led the way upstairs and into the master bedroom. She walked across to a large wardrobe fixture. She opened the double doors to reveal a long hanging space for dresses, and a short hanging space for blouses and skirts above a chest of four drawers. Mrs Wilson pulled the bottom drawer fully out. It was full of scarves, gloves and other occasional wear. She then tilted the drawer front upwards and pulled it towards her to remove it from its space. 'That's where my husband's Aunt Lilian kept her money and other valuables. Rachael Smith must have searched this room high and low. Perhaps she knew where to look.'

'Criminals do know where people keep

their valuables, Mrs Wilson. Beneath carpets and floorboards, on top of wardrobes, under the mattress, in pockets sewn into curtain valances, in the airing cupboard, in toilet cisterns, in spaces beneath drawers. They know,' confirmed Flora.

'It took us a few weeks to find this place. We found the house deeds, birth certificates and suchlike here. Thank goodness Rachael Smith didn't take any of those. I've something else to show you.'

They went downstairs. Mrs Wilson opened the front door. On either side was a cast iron decorative plant urn. Mrs Wilson pointed. 'How heavy would you think those are, filled with soil and planted as you see them now?' Noting Flora's look of speculation, she continued, 'Well, I'll tell you. They each weigh about three hundredweight.'

'About right, I suppose,' said Flora carefully, wondering what was coming next.

'We reckon that Aunt Lilian went to check on her money the night that she died.'

'Three hundred — '

'Let's not go there again,' interrupted Mrs Wilson. 'You are getting as bad as my Donald. I am quite certain that the money had been removed by Rachael Smith in preparation for her leaving Aunt Lilian. Probably during that night.'

'Go on,' urged Flora.

'I say that because the carpet had been cleaned just in front of the wardrobe. We reckon that Aunt Lilian had had a heart attack as a result of finding her money gone. We were told that vomiting often takes place with a heart attack. There was a roughened patch of carpet in front of the wardrobe where we think Aunt Lilian actually had her heart attack.' She paused, 'And Rachael Smith had cleaned it up instead of telephoning for an ambulance. You don't notice these things in a panic situation. Rachael Smith telephoned my husband to tell him that Aunt Lilian had had a heart attack and that she'd telephoned for an ambulance. We came here as quickly as we could and accompanied Aunt Lilian by following the ambulance to the hospital. She never recovered. My husband was livid. I thought he would follow his aunt that night with a heart attack of his own. He dismissed Rachael Smith on the spot. She drove off in a small van that she owned and we never saw her again.'

'And the significance of the urn?' Flora inquired.

'Several days later I noticed a rib of soil around the base of that urn. Donald instantly said, 'That pot has been moved.' He reckoned that Rachael Smith had hidden the money beneath it in case she was searched by the police. But of course that didn't happen.'

'And she came to retrieve it later.'

'Exactly,' replied Mrs Wilson. 'We tried to move the urn but it was too heavy for us to lift. Two lads from the local plant nursery moved it easily but there was nothing underneath.'

Just then, Essach and Donald Wilson joined Mrs Wilson and Flora at the front door.

'Thank you, Mrs Wilson, you've been a great help. We'll be in touch with you when we have made some more inquiries.' Flora waved as they left.

21

'So our prime suspect has at least two identities,' remarked Flora.

'And is possibly responsible for three deaths. We'd better find her asap, before she kills again. We'll go straight to Selby Park and check out that reference for a start.' Essach steered his car in that direction.

The address on the reference was at the end of a cul-de-sac. It was a three-storey semi-detached villa-style residence built during Queen Victoria's reign. The red brickwork had narrow mortar joints.

Essach remarked on the brickwork, 'Narrow mortar joints in those days to keep the bricks together.'

Flora looked at him quizzically.

'Not like today's builders. Mortar is cheaper than bricks, and so modern day brickies use wide joints to keep the bricks apart. More mortar, fewer bricks.'

'Your brain is full of useless information, Essach.'

Thinking of Rowena, Essach replied, 'Yes, I've been told that before. However, sometimes seemingly useless information helps me to solve murders.'

Beside the house was a smart, recently built, garage. Stone string courses, and stone window mullions and sills, indicated that it was an upmarket residence for its time, built to house the emerging middle class, such as a manager and his family, all those years ago. Essach and Flora rang the front doorbell. It was answered by a woman in her forties wearing a floral pinafore. The smell of baking hung around her.

Essach and Flora showed the lady their warrant cards.

'So, you've finally decided to leave your comfortable desks and investigate!'

Essach and Flora looked at each other.

'I'm sorry, madam, but are we at cross purposes here?' asked Essach.

'You've come about the peeping Tom burglar, haven't you?'

'Well, no, madam. We're making an investigation into a serious crime.'

'What? You mean that the peeping Tom burglar isn't a serious crime? How do you know we couldn't have all been murdered in our beds?'

'Let's start again,' suggested Flora, in a placating tone. 'You've had an incident which I expect your local police officers have investigated. We are investigating a serious crime which has actually happened in another locality. May we come in, please, and talk it through with you? Who knows, we might even be able to follow up the peeping Tom burglar incident.'

Reluctantly, the lady let them in and identified herself as Mrs Clarke. She led them through to the lounge at the rear of the house. It was comfortably furnished and had a double-door French window overlooking the garden, featuring a large ornamental pool. Flora noted that the marble fireplace was not as grand as that in Mr and Mrs Wilson's large house. Nor the cornices and ceiling roses as elaborate. There must have been coloured leaded-light windows before the plastic-framed double-glazed windows were installed. Mr and Mrs Wilson's Aunt Lilian had been more astute and retained hers, having secondary glazing installed.

'We're looking for a Mr Joseph Peat who used to run a building business from here, Mrs Clarke.'

'I'm sorry, but I don't know Mr Peat's whereabouts. I think he might be dead. My husband and I bought the house seven years ago. The sale was handled by Mr Peat's daughter who had power of attorney. Mr Peat had run his building business from here. As you can see, the garden widens out, and was used as a builder's yard.'

'You've made a very good job of restoring the garden then, Mrs Clarke,' said Essach admiringly.

'Mm. We've done everything except the pool. You should have seen the skip loads of brick ends and general rubble we had to get taken away. And then there were tons and tons of top soil delivered before we could even think of laying out flower beds.'

Flora noted Essach's sigh of impatience, but before she could get a word in edgeways, Mrs Clarke was off again.

'I understand from the neighbours that the daughter put the pond in, and it is rather too large to start altering. And about eight feet deep! We absorbed it as a feature of the garden. The daughter had power of attorney and my husband and I have wondered whether she needed that because her father was going gaga or something.'

'Can you recall the daughter's name, Mrs Clarke?' asked Flora.

'Yes. Her name is Rachael Smith. Mrs, though we never met her husband.'

Essach's and Flora's eyes met.

'You wouldn't know where Mrs Smith is now, by any chance, Mrs Clarke?' asked Flora hopefully.

'No. I can't help you there. I understand

124

that she went to work as housekeeper and live-in companion for a lady in Mafeking Road, after she'd sold this house to us. I can't help you with the number. But it wasn't too long after that, we heard that the lady had died. She was elderly and rumour had it that she'd left the house to Mrs Smith. Anyway, it was sold, and Mrs Smith must have moved away because I never saw her shopping locally after that.'

'Thank you, Mrs Clarke. You've been most helpful,' Essach gave her a grateful smile.

'And what about my incident?'

Essach and Flora listened to a long rigmarole of how someone had set the dog barking at a neighbour's house. They'd heard a splash, and their security lights came on. The Clarke's 8-year-old son had looked out of his bedroom window to see someone peering over the adjoining fence. Then he'd seen a tall figure, presumably a man, climb over the fence, run across the garden, and escape by climbing over the opposite fence. They'd called the police, who'd taken notes, but they'd heard no more.

Essach parked his car just inside Mafeking Road. It was made up of 'ribbon development' terraced houses, built at the same time as Mrs Clarke's house, similar, but more compact. Several cars were parked alongside the pavement, presumably outside each householder's own home.

'Nice hall floor in Mrs Clarke's house,' remarked Essach.

'Minton. Not much other original character left. Except the fireplace and decorative plaster work,' added Flora.

'We'd better inquire until we find the house that Rachael Smith lived in. You take this side and I'll cross over and knock on doors the other side.'

They were about halfway along the road when Flora struck lucky. She showed her warrant card to the lady who answered the door. 'I wonder if you could help me, please? I'm seeking information on a Mrs Rachael Smith, formerly Rachael Peat of Seventh Avenue. She used to live with her father, Joseph Peat, the builder.'

The householder studied her credentials and sized her up. 'Come in, please. I don't hold doorstep conversations.'

Essach saw Flora enter the house and the front door close behind her.

Flora followed the straight-backed figure, along a long hall to the second door, which she opened. Flora found herself in a similar but smaller room to the lounge that Mrs Clarke had taken Essach and her into. The French window gave a view of a blue brick paved yard running alongside a wing building with the garden commencing at the far end.

Essach decided not to join Flora; she was more than competent to interview the householder on her own. He returned to his car to find a piece of paper tucked behind his windscreen wiper. He carefully removed it and read in printed capitals, I DO NOT LIKE YOU PARKING YOUR CAR WHERE YOU LEFT IT. DO NOT DO IT AGAIN — OR ELSE. Essach snorted and then laughed out loud. He got into his car, put on a CD of Techung, read the note again and chuckled. Placing it on the dashboard he closed his eyes and meditated. At least they had found out a little more about Rachael Smith, alias Ruby Stone. He wondered what Flora might already be learning from the householder living on the opposite side of the road.

'This room is cosiest. Please make yourself comfortable while I make tea.' The white-haired lady fixed Flora with disconcertingly pale blue eyes. 'You sit in that armchair so that I will be facing you when we are talking.'

A spindle-backed cottage suite with squashy seat and back cushions took up most of the lounge. Flora sat in the almost straight-backed armchair as directed.

When the lady had left the room Flora looked about her. A shallow oak sideboard was placed against the hall wall behind the settee, and a drop-leaf table with barley twist legs stood beside the French window. Knitting occupied one seat of the settee. The fireplace was black with ivy leaf decoration painted on. Black slate, thought Flora. The painted ivy leaves were now faded and worn from several generations of house-proud housewives' dusting. A plain cornice ran around the ceiling.

The lady returned, moved the table to the centre of the room and raised and fixed one table-leaf in place. She then took a small embroidered cloth from the sideboard drawer and spread it over the table.

Trying to be polite, Flora said, 'I'm sorry. I don't know your name.'

'That's because you did not ask, Detective Sergeant Flora Hughes. Miss Church.' She emphasized the word, Miss. Leaving the room she returned with a tray containing elegant porcelain teacups, saucers, plates, matching teapot, sugar bowl, slop basin and milk jug. A stainless steel tea strainer took up a corner of the tray. Chocolate Olivers were spread on a doily on a larger plate. Miss Church handed Flora a tea plate containing a paper serviette. 'Milk, DS Hughes?'

'Yes, please,' Flora thanked her.

Miss Church handed Flora a cup of rather

milky tea. 'Please help yourself to sugar.' She indicated the bowl of coloured sugar crystals. 'Chocolate Olivers are there if you are not figure conscious. Now, how can I help you? You were asking about Rachael Peat.'

'We are trying to trace her, Miss Church. The new owner of the house in Seventh Avenue told me that Rachael Peat came to live in this road.'

'Two doors away. She lived with Mrs Priddy until Mrs Priddy died. After the house was sold I've no idea where she went.' She pursed her lips.

'Miss Church, you said that as if there was something you did not approve of.'

Miss Church winced. 'Indeed, I didn't approve. Elsie was as fit as I am. Just how did she catch pneumonia, is what I would like to know. Mrs Priddy was on her own. She had no family. When Rachael worked for her father, she specialized in working for ladies who preferred a woman rather than a man carrying out minor repairs and redecorating for them. Rachael did work for me as well, and very good she was too. The thing is, Mrs Priddy told me, in confidence, that Rachael had agreed to become her housekeeper and companion, in return for which she would receive free board and lodging and some spending money. But,' Miss Church knew how to keep the best of a good story until last, 'in addition, Mrs Priddy would leave her house to Rachael when she died.'

'That was not a very wise thing to agree to, Miss Church.'

'My feelings exactly. I told Elsie Priddy so. But by then, would you believe it, Rachael had insisted that Elsie sign some sort of document setting out their agreement.'

'But surely,' said Flora, between bites of her second Chocolate Oliver, 'no solicitor would have agreed to such a document!'

'Rachael knew what she was doing. Elsie Priddy let the proverbial cat out of the bag when she mentioned to me that she thought it was an option to purchase which she'd signed. I worked in the legal department of the local authority, so I do know the significance. No doubt Rachael registered the option against Mrs Priddy's house in the land charges registry to make it all legal and above board.'

'So that even if a distant relative had come on the scene, Rachael could have exercised her option to purchase?'

'Exactly. Rachael must have paid Elsie something for the option. It's called 'consideration' in the legal world, but it does not necessarily have to be much. Elsie never told me the amount. And to cap it all, Elsie died

130

of pneumonia. Pneumonia! I ask you. And the police not interested!'

'I'm sure you have a theory, Miss Church.'

'Damp bed sheets, DS Hughes. Damp sheets. The oldest trick in the business of getting hold of a rich relative's estate. Although Mrs Priddy was getting on a bit, probably in her mid seventies, she was the picture of health. She had everything to live for. I noticed Rachael putting bed sheets on the clothes-line the day before Mrs Priddy was taken to hospital.'

'You mean . . . ?'

'To dry out the damp sheets which Rachael had put on Mrs Priddy's bed and which had given her pneumonia.'

'That's a very serious accusation to make, Miss Church. Surely Mrs Priddy would have been aware that the sheets were damp, and so wouldn't have slept in the bed?'

'Rachael is a big strong woman, DS Hughes. She is well over six feet in height and has worked in the building trade all her life, lifting and carrying heavy loads. She could have tied up Mrs Priddy, or tucked the bed sheets in so tightly that she couldn't move or, she could have drugged her. Valium or suchlike in her bedtime drink. Rachael would then have delayed calling Mrs Priddy's doctor or, more likely, just called an ambulance.

Can't you imagine a woman in her middle seventies, delirious, and unable to answer questions lucidly? Anyway, Elsie Priddy died, and the house was sold. I have no idea where Rachael went from here.'

'How long ago was that, Miss Church. Can you recall?'

'It seems a long time. Six or seven years perhaps.'

'Thank you, Miss Church. You've been very helpful. One more question. Do you remember Rachael keeping a pencil on her person, please?'

'Yes. Now you come to mention it. She kept it behind her ear. To emulate where her father, Joseph Peat, kept his. It was always hidden, of course, beneath her lovely auburn hair. I'll tell you something else. Something I wouldn't say to any man. Rachael fainted at the sight of blood. She did it next door when she cut herself on a broken window pane which she was replacing. My neighbour called me to help her. I applied Mackenzies smelling salts to revive her while my neighbour, a retired nurse, cleaned the cut before putting on, is it called a butterfly or something like that, to pull the cut together. She then bandaged it so that there was no blood showing.'

As if reading Flora's thoughts, Miss

Church continued, 'Not good for a woman to be tickle-stomached or to faint at the sight of blood.'

Flora thanked her and left the house to rejoin Essach. She arrived at the car just as the resident of the house the car was parked outside came out. A middle-aged woman with a very red face demanded, 'Just how long do you intend to remain parked in front of my house? That's my husband's parking place and he'll be home soon. If you don't move I'll report you to the police.'

Essach and Flora looked at each other and, smiling, held up their warrant cards for the woman to see. She took a quick glance and an even quicker turn and bolted back towards her front door. Before she could close it behind her, Essach leaned across the passenger seat and out of the passenger door window he called, 'Prepare your husband for a visit from your local policeman. He'll want to see his driving licence, MOT, and insur — ' But the woman slammed the door on him.

'I reckon she had the last word,' remarked Flora.

'Women usually do,' replied Essach laconically. 'We'd better get back to the station before she reports us to the police. Kysoh — you've got to keep your sense of humour!'

22

Essach carefully wrote a letter of offer to Morels. First of all he thought he'd offer £90,001 for The Cottage. Then he thought he'd offer £91,000. But why should he? He'd stick strictly to the money his parents had given him to buy the house. He'd keep the savings which he and Rowena had accumulated in case of the proverbial 'rainy day'. They had intended to use it as their deposit on a one-bedroom flat of their own. Perhaps in West Ealing where it was possible to buy one for around £200,000. No, he'd offer £90,100, subject etcetera, etcetera.

★　★　★

'You have the authority from the Met to further your inquiries in the locality of, where is it?' asked Superintendent Salmone. 'Oh, yes, in the vicinity of 25 Friendship Road, Ealing. I've no need to remind you to exercise tact.'

'Not at all, sir. I'll question tactfully and carefully in all of my inquiries.'

Superintendent Salmone looked suspiciously at DI Wangdula, trying to detect any hint of sarcasm. 'I see from your most recent report that your prime suspect has two identities. You also report at least two suspicious deaths as well as two murders. A serial killer, do you think?'

'Very definitely, sir. I haven't yet had any leads on Joseph Peat; he seems to have just disappeared. And no information was volunteered on Rachael Smith's husband. We still have a lot more inquiries to carry out before we can successfully apprehend Rachael Smith, alias Ruby Stone, and secure a conviction. We'll get there, sir, I can assure you of that.'

'Well done, Detective Inspector Wangdula. I leave it in your capable hands.'

★　★　★

Flora sat beside Essach at his desk. 'We have plenty of leads now, Essach. Which one do we follow up first?'

'Consider me eccentric if you like, but I am interested in Rachael Smith's past. Miss Church spoke so highly of her when she was working for her father. What happened to make Rachael so callous? What turned her into a murderer? Where is her father, and where is her husband? Did she murder both of them too? We've already established in our own minds that Rachael Smith murdered Adrian Hill, and Israel Swindell-Banks, and is responsible for the deaths of Elsie Priddy and Mr and Mrs Wilson's Aunt Lilian. We have a serial murderer on our hands who has amassed a fortune and who could be out there, even now, murdering unsuspecting innocent people and adding to her wealth.'

'I don't see her murdering anyone else, Essach. With all that money Rachael Smith is sunning herself in France, or Spain, or Portugal, or Italy, or — '

'All right. I get your drift. But there are other places we need to explore for information. Young Mr Banks might be persuaded to fill in the blank as to what Rachael, alias Ruby Stone, and his father got up to. That something, which had such a profound effect on him, as to make him relinquish his almost guaranteed success in litigation with his father's housekeeper.'

'I've a feeling that he will be a hard one to crack,' replied Flora laconically.

'I wonder if we could track down which branch Rachael's father banked with? Joseph Peat seems to have been held in high regard. He lived in an expensive house for the district. He must have accumulated savings.

Just why didn't Rachael go to her father if she was desperate for money? Her resorting to murder tells us that she must have been desperate for cash.'

'Or her brain turned!'

'I suppose that is always a possibility.' Essach sat thinking for a moment. 'And then there is Rachael's bank when she was posing as Ruby Stone. When 25 Friendship Road was sold, her half-share was perfectly legitimate. She could prove its source and that it was not laundered. That money must be in a bank account somewhere. Nobody, not even a desperate murderer, would have over £1 million pounds lying about their home, would they?'

'Easy to check out. Lloyd Fisher gave us her solicitor's name and address. I'll ask them for information on her bank. I'll also ask for her last known address; not that she'll still be there. On the other hand her bank may have an up-to-date address.'

'While you are doing that I'll get on to Lloyd Fisher and ask him for the address of Mr Swindell-Banks junior. And, we don't know the purchasers' name; I'll need to contact them. To do that I'll need to go through their solicitors. At the same time I'll ask for their name and address.' Essach gave a sigh. 'We'll have to use a SOCO team with tact to find the proof we need to put Ruby Stone, whatever she calls herself, behind bars. As Mr MacMahon would say, 'You'll no be popular, Mr Wangdula'.'

They laughed together.

23

Essach felt his stomach give a little lurch as he read the letter from Morel's advising him that their clients had accepted his offer of £90,100 for The Cottage, Pestilence Lane, Baluster. He'd committed himself now. Honour would not allow him to go back on his word. The name, Pestilence, bothered him, but he supposed that it might be possible to have it altered some time in the future. He wrote a letter of acknowledgment to Morel's, and another to his parent's solicitors, Pink and Black, in London.

His parents would be pleased to hear that he had bought a house with the money they'd given him.

He set about looking through Yellow Pages for a firm of chartered building surveyors to carry out a survey of his prospective home.

★   ★   ★

'We have a reply from young Mr Swindell-Banks's solicitors. He does not want us to interview him. He says that that part of his life is behind him and is too painful to 'discuss,' stated Flora.

'Does he, now! I know what will change his mind,' stated Essach. 'Write to them again and say that we are investigating the suspicious death of Mr Israel Swindell-Banks, and that they and their client are obstructing further inquiries. As solicitors they will know the penalty for that.'

'I'll add to that letter that we would like to call on Mr Swindell-Banks junior next week. That should make them and their client sit up!'

Essach laughed. 'You're becoming as tactful as I am, Flora. In the meantime, the constable I gave the task of tracking down Joseph Peat's bank, has come up with a suggestion. The Regional and National Bank have a branch in Selby Park, close to where Mr Peat used to live. They have inquired if the retired manager can remember Mr Peat and his daughter, Rachael, and he says that he will be pleased to help out in any way that he can, without, however, breaching rules of client confidentiality.'

'Is he really going to be of help to us, do you think, Essach?'

Essach sighed. 'Worth a try, Flora. Let's go out now. Being retired, he's almost certain to be at home twiddling his thumbs.'

Essach drove them to Lode Hill, the

district adjoining Selby Park, to where Mr Whittaker, the retired branch manager of the Regional and National Bank lived.

On the journey they passed Lode Hill Cemetery behind iron railings, variegated laurels and ornamental trees. The dead of Baluster rested in the bright sunshine.

They parked the car on the drive of a post-war detached residence. There was space for several cars on the gravelled drive, with low shrubs on both sides. They rang the doorbell. After the third time, Flora said, 'I guess we'll have to come back another time. I'll push a note through the letterbox.' She wrote a brief note and folded it before posting it through the front door.

'Excuse me. Can I assist you?' They turned to find a middle-aged lady looking at them from the house on the right-hand side, from over the low growing shrubs.

'We just called on the off chance of seeing Mr Whittaker,' said Essach.

'We have Neighbourhood Watch here and I must tell you that I am not happy with people calling on the 'off chance', as you put it.'

'I congratulate you, madam,' replied Essach, taking out his warrant card. 'We are police.'

The lady screwed her eyes up the better to see. 'Hm. He's retired.'

'We know that, madam,' said Flora. 'That is why we called on the off chance. We thought that he'd be almost certain to be at home.'

The lady chuckled. 'You are living in the past, my dear. Retired people are just as active, or even more so, than the younger generation. Golf, bowls, touring, ballroom dancing, writing, painting, fishing. Oh, so many pastimes, so much so, that Mr and Mrs Whittaker do not spend that much time at home. Better come back this evening. After eight o'clock, mind you, as they dine out most evenings.'

'Thank you,' said Essach in an astonished voice.

As he drove back to headquarters, Essach asked, 'How are you fixed to return this evening, Flora?'

'Why not?'

'Then it's my turn to buy you a Chinese.'

It was just after eight o'clock when Essach and Flora arrived at the Whittakers' residence. There was no sign that they were at home. 'Hopefully, they've garaged their car and are at home!' said Essach.

Just then the front door was opened by a tall man with a straight back. He had a welcoming smile below his crisp moustache, and white hair to match. He wore a pale grey suit, a white shirt, a colourful tie and glasses of the latest shape. 'Mr Mangla?'

'Wangdula, actually, sir. Detective Inspector Wangdula, and my colleague, Detective Sergeant Hughes.'

'Ah, yes. My neighbour told me you'd called. Her sight is not all it should be and she's too vain to wear glasses. That's why she got your name wrong. Please come in.' He introduced them to Mrs Whittaker.

They both shook hands with her. She was shorter than her husband and was fussily dressed in a floaty skirt, blouse and shrug. 'Can I offer you a drink? Are you off duty this late in the day?'

Flora shook her head. 'A tea or coffee would do just as nicely, Mrs Whittaker.'

'You sit yourselves down on the patio with Sydney. I'll join you presently.'

'Now what is it I'm supposed to have done?' inquired Mr Whittaker.

'As far as we know, you are in the clear, Mr Whittaker,' Essach laughed. 'The truth is we need some help from you to clear up gaps in something that puzzles us.'

'Anything that I can do to help the police.'

'It concerns Rachael Smith and her father, Joseph Peat. Do you remember them, sir?'

'I remember. Mr Peat had his business account at the bank branch where I was manager. What ever happened to him; do you know?'

Just then Mrs Wittaker returned with four mugs of coffee on a tray. 'I do hope that you prefer thirsty mugs in preference to polite cups.'

Flora smiled her thanks as she and Essach accepted their welcome drinks.

'I'm afraid we can't help you there, Mr Whittaker. What can you recall that might be of interest or help to us, please? Also, do you know what happened to Rachael's father and to her husband?'

'Ah, Inspector! I don't know how much I can or should tell you. Client confidentiality and all that.'

'Please tell us everything, Mr Whittaker. I can't go into details as we too have to obey the rules of confidentiality. We are involved in a murder inquiry.'

Mr Whittaker let out a low whistle.

'It took place in London, but the evidence my colleague and I have uncovered so far, leads us to believe that Rachael is involved somewhere along the line.'

'And naturally, you want to clear her name.'

'Exactly, Mr Whittaker. Can you tell us what happened in the past, please?'

'Joseph Peat had a busy and prosperous

building and property repair business. His daughter, Rachael, worked with him and doted on him. Her mother died when Rachael was about 13 or 14. She took on the role of housekeeper to her father.'

At the word, housekeeper, Essach and Flora looked meaningfully at each other.

'Rachael loved working with her father. Had few outside interests.'

'Amateur dramatics, Sydney. Remember the pantomimes?' interrupted Mrs Whittaker.

'Ah! Those were the days! When our grandchildren were young enough for us to take them to pantomimes. Where was I? Oh yes, she was a strong girl. She was well over six feet in height. Taller than most men. Always had the knack of producing a pencil stub from behind her ear — both of which were normally out of sight beneath her thick auburn hair — when measuring timber, that sort of thing. Just like a conjuror. Let me think. She must have been about 22 or 23 when her father took on Jack Smith. He was well over six feet in height too. They seemed a perfect match and it was not long before they were married and living in the same house as Joseph Peat.'

'Was Rachael honest, Mr Whittaker?'

'Good heavens, yes! Honest as the day is long.'

'Was she violent in any way?'

'Good heavens, no. Whatever gave you that idea? Rachael was kind-hearted. She'd never hurt a fly. Why, when her father became ill, Rachael stayed at home to look after him while her husband, Jack Smith ran the business.'

'We've heard that Rachael became housekeeper to a Mrs Elsie Priddy. Why was that, Mr Whittaker. Did she fall on hard times?'

The retired bank manager sighed. 'While Rachael was tending to her father, problems occurred with the business.'

'Ah, problems. All God's children got problems, as my father often says. And then what happened?' asked Essach.

'It is getting a bit chilly out here. Let's go inside,' suggested Mrs Whittaker.

'We're sorry to take up so much of your time,' said Flora.

'No problem, my dear. I'm as interested as you are. Rachael and her father did work for us here, as well as at our previous home.'

They all followed Mrs Whittaker into the house where she went into the kitchen, carrying the tray of coffee mugs. Mr Whittaker led them into a spacious lounge where he switched on subdued lighting. 'The business went downhill,' continued Mr Whittaker. 'Gradually at first, and then

146

seriously. Jack Smith took to drink. Perhaps Rachael neglected him in favour of her father. I don't really know, it's just my theory. I never found out exactly what her father's illness was but it must have been serious. Anyway, Jack Smith was seen at the local bookies. Probably trying to win enough money to prop up the ailing business.'

'And so pushing it deeper into the red,' surmised Flora.

'Exactly. I allowed as much overdraft as I dare before telephoning Rachael and asking her to come in and see me.'

Mrs Whittaker rejoined them.

'What a sorry tale of woe. Joseph Peat's condition, whatever it was, Rachael didn't say, and I hadn't the heart to ask, was worsening. Her husband stayed at home that day to look after him while Rachael came to see me.'

'Not an easy day for you either, that day, eh, Sydney,' surmised Mrs Whittaker.

'Poor Rachael. Didn't know what had hit her. I explained as gently as possible the bank's dilemma. As the bank held the deeds of her father's house I suggested that her father used them as security if he needed to borrow more money. I didn't say anything about rumours I'd heard regarding her husband. Rachael surely must have known

147

about his drinking, and possibly about his gambling. She said she'd think about it.'

Flora couldn't help feeling sorry for Rachael until she remembered that it was her victims who deserved her pity.

'The next time Rachael came to see me, just a few days later, she said she and her father had come to the decision to sell the house and to move on, as she termed it,' continued the retired bank manager. 'Rachael told me that her husband, Jack, had absconded with what little money they had around the house. Another woman, Rachael supposed. Her father had gone into a home to be looked after on a permanent basis. She set up a direct debit to pay for his care.'

'So her father is still alive?' queried Essach.

'As far as I know, but the situation might have altered since I retired. Anyway, Rachael did as I suggested and borrowed some more money to make the house presentable for sale. I learned afterwards that she cleared the garden of all building materials, and dug out a deep pond, would you believe it?'

'Ah!' exclaimed Flora, 'we've seen that.'

'Joseph Peat's house was sold, but the money in the account was fast running out when Rachael inherited Mrs Elsie Priddy's house. Very fortunate, that. I don't know where the money would have come from to support Rachael's father if she hadn't inherited!'

'Do you know where Rachael went to from there, Mr Whittaker?'

'She became housekeeper to someone in Southfield, Detective Inspector, but I don't have the address. You could ask at my old branch of the bank. If you do, I'd rather you didn't mention my involvement, or that I have talked to you. My pension, you know. Bank directors are a breed apart, and can take a peculiar attitude to retired managers having spoken to the police, without having first consulted them for permission.'

'Surely not, Mr Whittaker. Bank directors can hardly consider themselves to be a special breed?'

'I'd rather not comment on that, Detective Inspector.'

All four of them laughed.

24

'At last. We now know for certain that the motive for all of the deaths is not just money.'

Flora frowned at Essach's statement.

'Filial piety.'

Flora remained silent.

'Rachael worships her father, and will do anything to ensure that he receives every available treatment for his illness. What else could possibly have motivated Rachael, a previously honest person with no history of violence, to take the lives of Elsie Priddy, Mrs Lilian Wilson, Mr Banks and Adrian Hill?'

Flora nodded.

'We have yet to establish what Mr Peat's illness is. I don't suppose for a moment that Rachael left her father in the same care home after she stole the £350,000. She'd be too canny for that. Just in case the police had decided to follow up on the missing money.'

'Anyway, she'd have moved her money to a bank in London, nearer to 25 Friendship Road. You can bet she's taken it all out since. So where is Rachael and her million pounds now?' asked Flora.

Essach read the report from Bentley's, the chartered building surveyors. Yes, he knew that The Cottage was at least 200 years old, and yes that it had been renovated to an acceptable standard some twenty to twenty-five years ago. Woodworm around the base of the first floor toilet pedestal; the electrician's report suggested complete rewiring. 'Huh,' said Essach to himself, 'good job that I don't need a mortgage. Both would have been conditions of the loan leading to complications. Still, I'll get the er, *anobium punctatum*, er, woodworm, treated.' The roof, guttering, secondary-glazed window frames, and walls all appeared to be up to standard and, to his surprise, there was no rising damp. The surveyor surmised that probably a chemical DPC had been injected during the renovation, and a guarantee given, but that would, no doubt, have expired by now.

The report ended with a caution that the name Pestilence Lane could inhibit any envisaged future sale of the property.

Essach wrote out a cheque in payment of the firm's account, and enclosed it in a thank you letter. He then wrote to Messrs Pink and Black requesting them to exchange contracts as soon as possible, with an early completion.

★ ★ ★

Techung's mellow voice filled Essach's car as Flora and Essach made their way to keep an appointment with Rachael Smith, aka Ruby Stone's solicitors.

'Do you really think their Mr Hayward will tell us very much?' asked Flora. 'He is going to plead client confidentiality.'

Essach sighed. 'Probably. I was aware at the outset of this case that it would be slow going, worming the necessary information out of people to solve this murder, and locate the proof needed to bring a successful prosecution.'

Essach parked the car in Hayward's private car park. They were led straight to Mr Hayward's office.

'If your inquiries have anything to do with the accidental death of the late Mr Israel Swindell-Banks, Detective Inspector, then you are wasting valuable police time.' Mr Hayward looked Essach in his almond eyes. 'Also, Mrs Ruby Stone is undoubtedly entitled to her half-share in the proceeds of the sale of 25 Friendship Road.' Before either Essach or Flora could comment, the solicitor took a deep breath and continued, 'In the first instance, police were standing outside the house and unable to gain access, when the accident happened inside the house. That proves it was an accidental death, pure and simple. As to how Mrs Ruby Stone came to own shared ownership in the property, I am not prepared to comment nor to speculate.'

'Even so, Mr Hayward, we have found evidence that Mr Swindell-Bank's death could have been the result of suspicious circumstances. If we could just have Mrs Stone's home address, please?'

'And,' added Flora, 'her bank details, please, sir.'

'Mr Hayward, you are being requested to assist the police in pursuing their inquiries,' added Essach.

Essach and Flora went to Brent to the address given to them, only to learn that Ruby Stone had vacated her flat over a year before and not left a forwarding address.

'No surprise there,' said Flora. 'Next stop coffee, and then to her bank.'

Essach murmured agreement.

Mr Craddock, the branch manager, remembered Mrs Stone extremely well. As he said, 'Well, not many depositors have over a million pounds in their bank account for a start, and never before or since has a depositor withdrawn the whole amount in ten and twenty pound notes.'

Startled by Mr Craddock's matter of fact

statement, Essach asked, 'Is it possible to do that, Mr Craddock?'

'Given sufficient notice, yes. Mrs Stone did give the bank the necessary notice. I obviously tried to persuade her to invest the money in a bond but she would have none of it.'

'But how? I mean, what does a million pounds look like, Mr Craddock?'

The bank manager laughed. 'She didn't draw it all out in one go, Detective Inspector. Mrs Stone withdrew her money over five occasions; not advisable for anyone to handle a quarter of a million on our streets. I advised her against it.'

Flora broke the silence that followed, 'Just how did Ruby Stone carry that amount of money, Mr Craddock?'

The bank manager turned to Flora. 'You may well ask. She had a sort of double-sized shopping trolley. Once it had been filled in the privacy of this office, Mrs Stone placed grocery packets she'd brought with her, on top of the money to conceal it, and protruding to give the impression that it was full of groceries. My staff and I were absolutely fascinated. Then she used her mobile phone to call for a taxi. On her fifth visit she closed her account and we never saw her again.'

'I don't suppose you have a home address for her, sir?' Flora pleaded more in despair than in hope. The bank manager gave them the address in Brent at which they'd already drawn a blank. They were at a dead end.

25

'At least we know Rachael Smith is still in this country if her father is still alive. She must visit him on a regular basis,' said Essach.

'But we don't know if he is still alive. If he isn't, then Rachael could be sunning herself in Spain or some other hot country.'

'Well, we do have an identikit picture of her, which Mr Wilson recognized. We could send that to Interpol with a good description of her. We'll catch up with her. But before we do I'd rather like to obtain the proof that she murdered Mr Israel Swindell-Banks at 25 Friendship Road.'

'Who knows, the son, Mr Swindell-Banks junior, could have a photograph of his father's housekeeper? I'll confirm arrangements for us to visit him.' Flora busied herself organizing their visit.

★　★　★

Looking for David Swindell-Bank's house, Flora noticed a synagogue. Obviously they were in a residential district with a predominant Jewish population. She knew that Jews are expected to walk to their nearest place of worship, so it made sense to live in the locality of a synagogue. They came to a post-war detached red brick house and were met at the door by a smartly dressed woman in her late thirties.

'Detective Inspector, I can't see where your interviewing my husband can lead to. The death of my father-in-law has upset him very badly.'

'Mrs Swindell-Banks. We are in possession of new evidence which leads us to believe that your father-in-law's death was a suspicious death. Who knows, if we can prove that a crime was committed, your husband could be entitled to claim back a considerable sum of money. In UK law, a criminal is not entitled to benefit from a criminal activity.'

'Just a minute, please.' Mrs Swindell-Banks left Essach and Flora standing on the front doorstep.

Flora pointed to a small elongated metal container on the doorframe. 'A mezuzah,' she just had time to say before David Swindell-Banks came to the door.

'Please come in.' He led them to a comfortable sitting room where his wife stood waiting for them to enter. 'Please take a seat.' He cocked his head to one side. 'Now what's this I hear, that you have fresh evidence that my father's death is suspicious? You mean that it might not have been accidental? Why haven't I been told about this? Don't you think I should have the right to know? I'll speak to my solicitors about this. And to your superior officer,' he added, glaring at Essach.

'We are looking for further evidence, Mr Swindell-Banks. That's why we are here.'

'What further evidence? There is no further evidence. I was actually outside 25 Friendship Road when my father fell down the stairs. It had to be an accident. What else could it have been?'

'Can you tell us why your father made over half of the value of his house to Mrs Stone, please?'

'No, I can't,' David Swindell-Banks snapped back.

'Can't or won't, Mr Swindell-Banks?' Essach replied quietly.

'Excuse me. I think I heard the girls.' Mrs Swindell-Banks rose from her chair.

Flora followed her. 'Mrs Swindell-Banks, I wonder if I could use your . . . ' she closed the door behind her.

'All right. I won't tell you.'

'Please allow me to confirm, Mr Swindell-Banks, that anything you tell me will be held in strictest confidence.'

'You are very naïve, Detective Inspector, if

you think I'd fall for that old chestnut.'

'Mr Swindell-Banks, should we find proof that your father was murdered in a particularly clever manner and, believe me, we shall find that proof if it still exists, then the motive behind his murder will be crucial to obtain a conviction.'

'What proof?'

'I'm not in a position to divulge that information at this delicate stage in our inquiries. Sorry about that, Mr Swindell-Banks.'

'Hah! Moonshine. There is no proof, because his death was accidental and, quite frankly, that is how I prefer that it should remain. An accidental death.'

'If we can prove that your father's death was murder, and if the murderer benefited financially from the crime, then you will have a case to sue for the return of over a million pounds.'

David Swindell-Banks narrowed his eyes. 'You mean my father's housekeeper, Mrs Ruby Stone?'

'Yes. Ruby Stone is our prime suspect.'

'What does she have to say about your accusation?'

'We haven't located her, as yet, to question her, Mr Swindell-Banks.'

'What a farce! Don't even bother looking any more. You'll get no help from me, even if you do catch up with Mrs bloody Ruby Stone.'

'I'm surprised that you didn't challenge her in the courts, Mr Swindell-Banks. Who knows, the police might have been alerted sooner to her motive in coercing your father into parting with his ownership of half such a valuable residence!'

'That's enough, Detective Inspector. You are seeking to delve into what is a very private family matter. You'll get no more information from me. Where's your colleague got to? I think it is time that you both left my home. I am asking you to go.'

'Very well,' said Essach. 'Let's find Detective Sergeant Flora Hughes and we'll take up no more of your time.'

* * *

Flora left the spotless cloakroom and made for where she thought the kitchen might be. She came to a door from behind which she could hear voices. She knocked and opened the door. 'May I please come and join you? My boss and your husband seem to be in a heated argument and I really don't want to be a part of it.'

'Is police work always like this?' asked Mrs Swindell-Banks.

'Not always, but from time to time it does have its moments.'

'These are my daughters, Ruth and Rebecca.'

The girls, aged about 12 and 14 said, 'Hello,' and continued drinking their tea and eating cake.

'Is this about Granddad falling downstairs?' asked Ruth. 'And Ruby Stone getting all that money?' added Rebecca.

'Would you like a cup of tea, er? Sorry I've forgotten . . . '

' . . . My name? It's Detective Sergeant Flora Hughes.'

The two girls looked suitably impressed.

Flora noticed that Mrs Swindell-Banks had avoided answering her daughters' questions.

'Why wouldn't Daddy let us have some of Granddad's toy houses to play with?' asked Rebecca.

'Eat your cake,' replied her mother.

'I'm sorry not to offer you cake, Detective Sergeant. We Jews can drink with those who are not of our faith but we are strictly forbidden to eat with them. I hope that you will understand.'

'Perfectly, Mrs Swindell-Banks,' Flora reassured her. 'Actually, I've been reading up on Jewish customs. I found out that you all have a very interesting background.'

'Granddad used to eat with Mrs Stone,' said Ruth.

'And she wasn't Jewish,' added Rebecca.

'Granddad was Granddad,' said Mrs Swindell-Banks, 'But your father and I stick to the old traditions.'

'I saw Mrs Stone in Kew Gardens last year on our school outing,' said Ruth. 'She was pushing an old man in a wheelchair. I wonder if he was her granddad?'

Just then David Swindell-Banks came into the kitchen. 'Ah! There you are. Your colleague is ready to go now.'

Flora drank the last of her tea and followed him out into the hall.

★　★　★

They were travelling back to Baluster when Flora decided to open the conversation before Essach fed the disc of Techung he held in his hand into the CD player.

'How did you get on with Mr Swindell-Banks?'

Essach fed the disc into the player but turned the volume down low.

'No joy whatsoever. He wouldn't reveal why his father gave Ruby Stone half of the ownership of 25 Friendship Road. Whatever they got up to it had to be of a scandalous nature. And you? I saw you slyly make a tactful exit!'

'Two things. The Swindell-Banks's two daughters were in the kitchen. Both youngish. Might just be teenagers. Anyway, they let slip two snippets of information. One, that Ruby Stone was seen last year pushing an old man in a wheelchair around Kew Gardens. And two, that Mr Swindell-Banks senior had some toy houses.' Flora stopped for effect.

'Go on.'

'And Mr David Swindell-Banks wouldn't let his own daughters have any of them to play with!'

Essach turned the volume down even lower on Techung. 'If Rachael was pushing her father around Kew Gardens in a wheelchair then he must have been resident in a nearby care home or some such.'

'My thoughts exactly.'

'But toy houses? Were they model houses, I wonder? Either way, why did he have them, and what was so special about them that his own son wouldn't allow his granddaughters to have them? I wonder what happened to them?'

'Burned,' said Flora laconically. 'What else? If they were evidence of something that Mr Swindell-Banks junior wanted to keep secret, there would be no better way to dispose of them. There's no safer way of destroying evidence than burning it.'

'Before I forget, what was that word you used before Mr Swindell-Banks asked us in?'

'Mezuzah?'

'That's the one.'

'That oblong thing on the doorframe. That's called a mezuzah.'

'Go on,' urged Essach.

'It is a sort of reminder as far as I can make out. To remind the occupants of the house to love God and to keep the Ten Commandments.'

'Not a bad idea,' approved Essach. 'We don't get many Jewish criminals. Maybe it should be made law to have something of the sort nailed to everyone's front doorpost!'

26

Essach read the letter from Messrs Pink and Black saying that they had arranged to exchange contracts on The Cottage and complete on the same day. He then looked at their account. Stamp duty, searches, land registry charges, et cetera, et cetera. He gasped. Added to the £90,100 price agreed for the cottage, there would not be much left of his £100,000 fund.

Essach looked at his miniature compass cufflinks, located the direction of Tibet, positioned himself so that he faced, more or less, in the direction of Lhasa, and meditated.

The first thought that came into his head, was that he'd done this so many times recently, that he already knew where Tibet lay in relation to his police quarters, but it had become habit-forming.

He closed his eyes and prayed to his great, great, great grandparents who, he knew, had owned property in Lhasa. When he opened his eyes they came to rest on an envelope which had arrived with the letter from Pink and Black. The Salvation Army logo was printed on the outside of the envelope. The thought popped into his mind that he could always leave the cottage to the Salvation Army on his death; make a new will and leave it to them to either find a use for it, or sell it and use the money to help people caught up in natural disasters, or with problems, or with . . . Yes, that is what he'd do.

Essach telephoned Mr Pink and avoided asking him how he was. He'd already done that and received the reply, 'In the pink, thank you.' They arranged for money to be electronically transferred into Pink and Black's clients' account, and for the completion to take place during the following week. If possible, within three days.

★ ★ ★

'I've located a very upmarket care home within easy walking distance of Kew Gardens. However — '

'There always seems to be a 'however', Flora, in this murder case. However what?'

'Joseph Peat died a natural death late last year. He'd been suffering from dementia. I explained that it is important we contact the next of kin to overcome the normal confidentiality reticence.'

'And?'

'The same address that Rachael Smith,

166

aka, Ruby Stone, gave to her solicitors and bank.'

'Well, thank goodness there is at least one natural death in our serial murderer's life.' Essach scratched an itch on his nose. 'There's more isn't there, I can tell. I feel that I now know you well enough, Flora.'

'Well, yes. But I've been instructed not to tell you. The super wants to tell you himself.'

Just then a WPC came to Essach's desk and placed a note on it. Essach read, 'Would like to talk to you asap in my office.' It was signed 'Salmone'.

Essach felt a cold chill run down his spine. 'I'm in trouble. I've had this type of note from my superior when I was attached to the Met. It always spelt trouble.'

Flora made no comment.

Essach picked the note up and went to Superintendent Salmone's office door. He knocked.

'Come.'

'Ah! There you are, Wangdula. From reports handed to me, you and DS Hughes seem to be making progress with this murder investigation. But macrophilia? I don't like the sound of that!'

'Macrophilia, sir! What is macrophilia? It sounds like some sort of begonia!'

Superintendent Salmone read from a

document on his desk.

'Sexual fantasy involving domination by giants.'

Essach looked puzzled.

'Rachael Peat, Smith, Ruby Stone. Whatever she's calling herself at the moment. She's a giant, isn't she?'

'I suppose she is, sir.'

'There's more to it than that. Apparently it often involves creating a Lilliputian world using model buildings, but leads to, er, happenings, that are so unpleasant to talk about that I am not prepared to discuss them in detail. No wonder David Swindell-Banks wants his late father's activities kept under wraps. This information is not really essential to your investigations, surely?'

'W-e-l-l.'

'I thought not. Find your proof linking this giant of yours to the murder of, of . . . ' he searched amongst papers on his desk.

'Adrian Hill, sir?'

'Ah, yes. Adrian Hill. We've got prostitution off the streets in Baluster, and we keep a tight rein on known paedophiles. Our vice squad have everything under control. The last thing wanted in Baluster is even a breath of macrophilia in the local press. Concentrate on Adrian Hill's murder. Got that, Wangdula?'

'Yes, sir.'

'Good man. I won't detain you any longer.'

Essach returned to his desk where Flora was seated, waiting for him.

'Am I allowed to ask?' Flora raised her eyebrows.

'Macrophilia. I'd never heard of it before. I suppose it is the reason why Mr Swindell-Banks senior made Ruby Stone joint owner of his valuable house.'

'My fault. I quite innocently put 'gigantism' into my computer. I was just reading all about macrophilia fetishes when the vice squad came down on me like the proverbial ton of bricks. Said that I shouldn't have been able to access such an inappropriate site. I replied to her, that if that was the case, someone had been negligent in not having the site programmed as inaccessible. That upset that hard faced — '

'Flora!'

'Well she is. Anyway, when she gave me time to explain, she did have the grace to tell me some of the things people get up to when practising macrophilia. And before you ask, I'm not telling you, it's so horrible. But it is definitely why David Swindell-Banks will never tell you. It was obviously what Ruby Stone and his father got up to. Maybe Ruby Stone took a video or secret photographs of their activities? Whatever. She had a strangle-hold on her employer.'

'An unfortunate turn of phrase, Flora. Applied to the murderer of Adrian Hill, that is.'

'We've both been put in our place this morning, Essach, so what next?'

'Do we have the name of the purchasers of 25 Friendship Road yet?'

'No. I've written to their solicitors but have not received a reply up to now.'

'Time to get heavy with them, Flora. Please give them a call — obstructing police with their inquiries. We need names and a telephone number. While you do that, I'll find out how and if it is possible to drill or hollow out a newel post.'

27

Essach walked the relatively short distance from police headquarters to Bentleys, the chartered building surveyors' offices. He'd remembered a Graham Winton had signed the survey report on The Cottage.

'Good morning. Is Mr Graham Winton in, please?'

The receptionist asked, 'Do you have an appointment, sir?'

'No. But I am a client.'

'And what is your name, sir?'

'Detective Inspector Essach Wangdula.'

'And the property involved, sir?'

'The Cottage, Pestilence Lane.'

With a scarcely concealed smirk, the receptionist said, 'I'll go and see if Mr Winton can spare a minute to see you.'

While she was gone Essach looked around the reception area at the red and white ranging poles, old fashioned looking theodolites and long-linked chains on display and framed photographs of cracks in buildings, rot-infected timbers and ancient land plans on the walls. A measuring rod was labelled, 'Sopwith staff, circa 1875.'

The receptionist returned, her pale grey eyes now serious. 'Mr Winton asked if there is a problem with his survey, sir.'

'No. None that I am aware of. I merely wanted to ask his advice on a problem we have in solving a crime.'

The receptionist gave Essach a relieved smile. 'I'm sure Mr Winton would be happy to offer any help that he is able to give. I'll show you through to his office.' She led the way to a light and airy office at the rear of the building. 'Detective Inspector Wangdula would like you to give him some advice in solving a crime, Mr Winton.'

Graham Winton rose and shook hands with Essach. 'Welcome, Detective Inspector. How can I be of service to you?' His handshake was firm, and he smiled out of the healthy ruddy face usually associated with a farmer. Essach judged him to be well into his sixties.

They both sat at the Victorian partners' pollard oak desk; Essach on the opposite side to the surveyor. Behind Graham Winton was a large drawing board beneath a wide window. Above it a suspended long neon light hung, and a spotlight was clipped to the top edge of the board.

Around the walls were shelves on which were arranged samples of bricks, roofing and floor tiles, copper and brass plumbing joints and items in clear plastic bags. These were tightly sealed, from what Essach could see of them, and numbered.

'I see that you have been observing our own 'Black Museum', Detective Inspector. The bags are tightly sealed so that the spores of dry rot do not escape. In the old days when trouser turn-ups were in fashion we surveyors used to joke that it was mainly us who spread the fungus. Good for business. I once told it to a householder who wouldn't be convinced that it was only a joke.' He looked at Essach's inscrutable almond eyes and coughed. 'Ah, well, what can I do to help you?'

'I'm looking for evidence for how a crime could have been committed, Mr Winton.'

'I know all about evidence, Detective Inspector. Look around you. All of those samples are evidence of some defect or other. My job is somewhat similar to yours. Inspect a property; look for any defects — subsidence, rising damp, rot, leaking radiators.'

'Woodworm?'

'Ah, yes. There is woodworm at The Cottage, isn't there? Buy a Rentokil injector. Treat it yourself, unless, of course, you want a guarantee. Now, how can I be of help to the police?'

Essach explained how he thought a hypothetical murder could have been carried out by concealing a tripwire inside a newel post.

'Hypothetical, you say?'

'At this stage, yes. And will you please keep our conversation confidential.'

'Most everything my work involves must remain confidential, Detective Inspector.'

'Thanks.' Essach continued to explain how he thought such a tripwire could be set up. He asked for a sheet of paper and made a rough sketch of what he had in mind. 'But could a newel post some five or six feet long be hollowed out to accommodate a two-inch nail?'

'Hm. Yes, it could be done. But I think the longest drill bit on the market is likely to be one metre long, thirty-nine inches. The newel post would have to be drilled from both top and bottom if it were longer than thirty-nine inches.'

'And the diameter?'

'Oh, I would say fifteen or sixteen millimetres would accommodate a two-inch nail head.'

'Just how difficult would it be to remove the knobs from the ends of the newel post?'

'We call them knops or bosses in the trade. Some are glued into place, others screwed, some screwed and glued, and in cheaper jobs, just nailed. Depends.'

'But somebody brought up in the building trade would know what to do?'

'Very definitely. A good workman would know what to look for and should cause hardly any damage, or none at all.'

'Thank you, Mr Winton. You've told me all that I need to know. Perhaps one day fairly soon you'll hear about why I needed your expert information. Thank you once again.'

As Graham Winton opened his office door for Essach to leave, he said, 'By the way, I noticed the caravan in the orchard adjoining The Cottage when I carried out my survey. Might I suggest that you do all that you can to persuade the occupant to decamp and camp somewhere else? Lowers the tone of the neighbourhood.'

'Even in Pestilence Lane?'

'You have a point there, Detective Inspector. However, you could go for a name change some time in the future. Perhaps from Pestilence Lane to Happiness Lane. Just a thought. Anyway, be happy in your new home.'

28

'Any luck?' asked Essach, as he approached Flora's desk.

'The new owners of 25 Friendship Road are prepared for us to interview them this evening. Their solicitor will be there, and he asks that we are tactful with our questions. And — '

'Yes?'

'Knowing our suspicions, not to mention the phrase, 'suspicious death'.'

'We'll be tactful. Our inquiries will be in general terms only. What time this evening, Flora?'

'I've arranged for us to meet at six o'clock.'

'I'd better inform Superintendent Salmone.'

Essach went to his own desk and phoned his superior officer's secretary and asked for an appointment. Presently his telephone rang. 'Superintendent Salmone will see you in an hour's time.'

'Thank you.'

Essach busied himself reducing what seemed an Everest of paperwork, to Cotswold proportions. It was just like the spam filtered out on his laptop, and which he never, ever opened. It was always deleted. A fair proportion of his paperwork met a similar fate by being consigned to the waste paper basket.

His internal telephone rang.

'Wangdula.'

'Ah! I'm ready to see you, if you'd come immediately.'

'Yes, sir.'

Essach tapped politely on the open door leading into Superintendent Salmone's office and entered, closing the door behind him. 'Two things, sir. I want to bring you up to date with our inquiries in the Adrian Hill and Israel Swindell-Banks murders.'

Superintendent Salmone's eyes narrowed.

'Detective Sergeant Hughes and I are meeting the purchasers of 25 Friendship Road this evening, with their solicitor in attendance. General questions only at this stage. I'll be very tactful.'

The Superintendent winced. 'I thought — '

'Yes, sir,' Essach hastily added. 'General questions only. If the new owners have had redecorating and or improvements carried out at Friendship Road since moving in, the proof which is essential to our case on both murders may no longer exist. I can assure you, sir, that my questions will be only in general terms. I have already promised not to mention the phrase 'suspicious death'.'

'Well . . . '

'And I have already established how Mr Swindell-Banks could have fallen to his death while Mrs Ruby Stone was outside the house.' He explained his theory that the newel post had been hollowed out to secrete a trip wire, and that he had had the possibility confirmed by a chartered building surveyor. 'However,' he continued, 'the conclusive proof will come from the remaining piece of gardening twine if it is still behind the first floor landing skirting board.'

'And if you find out that it has been removed during maintenance work?'

'I doubt whether the public prosecutor will support taking an action against Rachael Smith, sir. We should then just have to hope that she does not strike again.'

'Alright. And the second.'

'Sir?'

'You mentioned a second request.'

'Oh, yes. I shall be completing on a house that I've bought in three days' time. I would like to have either next week, or the week after, as part of my holidays, in order to move in.'

'Holidays? You've been here hardly five

minutes and you are talking about taking a holiday!'

'Only to move into my new home, sir. By buying a house it does mean that I have committed myself to remaining in Baluster, sir.'

'Quite so, quite so. As a matter of interest, what will be your new address, Detective Inspector Wangdula?'

'The Cottage, Pestilence Lane, Baluster, sir.'

'Ah! Well! I hope that you are soon settled in comfortably and will be happy in your new home. You'll let me know which week, won't you.'

'Yes, sir.'

⋆   ⋆   ⋆

Essach drove up the drive in front of 25 Friendship Road and parked his car behind a black BMW. A man emerged from the driver's seat of the BMW and met him and Flora.

'Stanley Parton.' He held out his hand and shook Essach's and then Flora's hand. 'Mr and Mrs Bullock's solicitor.'

Essach introduced themselves.

The solicitor turned to Flora. 'Ah, yes. It was you I spoke to earlier on. Mr and Mrs

Bullock will not impede inquiries, providing they are of a general nature only. Mrs Bullock is of a sensitive disposition. She is on edge at the moment as their daughter is due to give birth any day now.'

Flora showed her feminine side with the sparkle in her eyes.

Mr Parton rang the doorbell. Mr Bullock opened the front door. The solicitor introduced Essach and Flora to him. Mr Bullock led them through the house and into the rear garden where he introduced them to Mrs Bullock. Mrs Bullock was slim, despite being middle aged. Her face looked drawn and strained. She sat at a metal table, with a mobile telephone and a tall glass, side by side, on it. By contrast, her husband was running to fat with a roll of flesh sitting on his shirt collar. All three men wore ties despite the humid weather.

On the garden table stood a jug of fruit drink, and three drinking glasses on a tray. On the opposite side of the table, a part-filled glass, indicated where Mr Bullock had been sitting.

'Draw up chairs, please,' Mr Bullock invited. 'Glass of mango and tangerine?' At a nod from all three visitors, he poured three glasses and handed them out. 'Now, what is this all about?'

Essach replied. 'When the late Mr Swindell-Banks had his accident, two of our police officers attended. It is our job to double check the facts just in case the reports produced by our officers are ever disputed.'

Flora gave a covert stern look towards Essach at his plausible lie.

Stanley Parton visibly relaxed.

'Disputed?' echoed Mr Bullock.

'Life insurance. That sort of thing. Mr Swindell-Banks's unfortunate accident.'

'Ah!' Mr Bullock expressed his understanding. 'Just what information would be relevant, Detective Inspector?'

'We would like to have a look around, if we may. But first, have you carried out any alterations since moving into your new home?'

Mr Bullock shook his head. 'No. No alterations.'

'Redecorating then?'

'Oh, yes. Lounge, master bedroom, guest bedroom, hall, landing and staircase.'

'Kitchen,' added Mrs Bullock.

'We had only a brief glimpse as we came through, Mr Bullock. Would you favour us with a tour, please?'

'Certainly.' As with anyone who'd just moved into their latest home, Mr Bullock was delighted to show Essach and Flora around.

Mrs Bullock picked up the mobile telephone, and all five of them moved towards the house. Mrs Bullock led them into the kitchen. There, Flora and Essach could not help giving a gasp of awe.

'My Metris kitchen. I've always wanted one.' Mrs Bullock waved her hand to expressively take in the wavy lines of the charcoal and white units; the side by side inset stainless steel sink units; the concealed lights, which Mrs Bullock manipulated, including a ring of them beneath the edge of the circular table.

'It is beautiful,' gasped Flora.

Mrs Bullock gave a strained smile. 'I'm glad you like it. My husband will show you over the rest of the house. I'm expecting an important telephone call. I'll be in the garden if you need me.'

When Mrs Bullock had left the kitchen, her husband switched off the lights. 'Cost a lot of money, but you get what you pay for, and we are both more than just happy with it; we're ecstatic. I'll show you around the rest of the house.' Mr Bullock led the way to the lounge, dining room, cosy sitting room, study and upstairs to see the bedrooms on two floors. Everywhere there were plastic container scented air fresheners, and everywhere was immaculate.

Essach and Flora were on the alert in case their host should say anything which might assist them with their inquiries. They stopped at the head of the flight of stairs which led to the ground floor. Essach covertly looked at the newel post and at the skirting opposite for any signs of the alleged woodworm hole and the open joint where the skirting and the stringboard met. Both were invisible. They had been dealt with expertly.

Inwardly Essach groaned, but he looked admiringly about him. 'I must congratulate you on your choice of decorating firm. They have done a wonderful job. Very pleasing.'

'Ah! That's Lancashires for you. Top quality job,' replied Mr Bullock.

'Only as a matter of interest, Mr Bullock, could we have a walk around your garden? From just what little I could see when we were sitting around the garden table, it is worth admiring.'

Flora's eyes rose beneath her eyelids at Essach's pandering to any proud home owner's instincts.

They walked across the lawn and along the paths at a gentle pace.

'Did you have to do much to the garden to get it to your liking, Mr Bullock?' asked Flora.

'Not really. That bed over there was empty.

It looked as though it had been recently dug and the soil turned over; so I planted heathers. But as you can see, they haven't grown very well.'

They all looked at the forlorn heathers. Some were very obviously dead.

'You're always likely to suffer casualties, of course,' remarked Mr Bullock.

'Try forking peat into the soil, Mr Bullock. Perhaps it is not acidic enough,' advised Stanley Parton.

'I'll do that, Stanley. Thanks for the tip.'

Essach and Flora made their farewells leaving Stanley Parton to mull over the waste of police time he and his clients had just witnessed.

29

The following day found Essach and Flora back in Ealing. 'I am quite certain that neither Mr Bullock nor Stanley Parton knew what we were looking for, but we mustn't take any chances.'

Flora nodded agreement. They were sitting in one of the SOCO white vans, two roads away from Friendship Road. Figures dressed in white sat around the van, trying to keep cool, on what promised to be another hot August day. One of them sat beside a computer and printing machine waiting to print out a search warrant.

'I'm just not happy about producing a photocopy of a search warrant. We are supposed to produce the real thing. Say, for instance, if by some chance, Stanley Parton just happened to be at the house when we attempted to serve it?'

'We'd recognize his BMW. Easy enough to check the registration number with the DVLA in Swansea. I'd have to find some story to distract his attention while you explained to, hopefully, Mrs Bullock, and obtained her consent.'

'You are good at finding stories to suit the occasion, aren't you, sir? You were very good last night.'

A slight nudging of elbows between white clad figures did not escape Flora's notice. 'Not what you think, lads. Pure thoughts, have pure thoughts.'

'Alan Lancashire has agreed to see me at eleven o'clock, Detective Sergeant Hughes.' They were always formal with each other in the presence of other police officers. 'Hopefully, his firm's account to Mr Bullock for redecorating will tell me all that I need to know. I've warned him that my visit must be kept on a strictly confidential basis, but we're taking no chances. I didn't tell him what it is about.'

'Thanks for putting me in charge of the SOCO team's visit to 25 Friendship Road, sir. We're all prepared and can be off at a moment's notice. I'm getting goose bumps just thinking about it.'

'You'll be all right. You know what we're looking for. Mr and Mrs Bullock don't. Just be ready,' Essach turned to the SOCO team, 'to get to 25 Friendship Road at a moment's notice. My gut feeling is that the element of surprise is essential here. Mr Bullock is a wealthy man and protective of his wife.' He turned back to face Flora. 'Did you see the tender way that he looked at her? He could quite easily subvert our intentions if he had even an inkling of what we are looking for.'

'You're getting paranoid now, sir.'

'I don't think so. It is my opinion that he wanted that house more than she did. A death had occurred there. Look what he must have spent on the kitchen! That must have cost a whole shed full of money.'

Flora sighed. 'A dream kitchen. Worth every penny I'd say.'

'I'd say that it was a bribe. In one context it is almost as bad as blackmail. Just what is it about that house?'

'Hm. You might be right there. I'd like to bet you that Stanley Parton turns up.'

'No bet. You'd win,' chuckled Essach. 'Better use plenty of sheeting to protect the property. Mrs Bullock seems to be over zealous with her house cleaning and deodorants. Right. I hope that the super has obtained the search warrant by the time I telephone you. I'd better get off now otherwise I'll be late for my appointment.'

★   ★   ★

'Welcome, Detective Inspector. What can I do for you?' Alan Lancashire held his hand out

187

and shook Essach's vigorously. 'Please take a seat.'

'I have a favour to ask you, Mr Lancashire.'

'Please, do go on.'

'During the last year or so, your firm carried out fairly extensive decorating at 25 Friendship Road, Ealing.'

Alan Lancashire frowned. His face was already crinkled and the effort of memory gave his face a look of crêpe paper. 'Aha. I remember now. The house where the owner fell down the stairs. Is that the one?'

'That's the one, Mr Lancashire.'

Alan Lancashire smiled, giving him a disarming, impish look. 'Mr George Bullock employed us. Big man. Big in the stock broking market. Yes. I do remember. He'd had a state of the art kitchen installed. Mr Bullock showed it to me. He locked the door so that my men couldn't wander into it while working there.'

Essach smiled. 'That's the gentleman, Mr Lancashire.'

'What's he done, Detective Inspector Wangdula? You mentioned confidentiality in your telephone call this morning.'

Essach avoided answering that question by asking a question of his own. 'Could I have a look through the firm's invoices with regard to the work carried out there, please?'

'But why? Everything was above board, I can assure you.'

'For reasons of confidentiality, I cannot divulge why, at this stage, Mr Lancashire. But I can say that neither your firm nor Mr Bullock are under suspicion of any offence. May I see those invoices, please?'

'Well, I don't know. I'll have to consult with my client.'

'Mr Lancashire! What do either you or Mr Bullock have to consider? You've nothing to hide. You've committed no offence.'

'Well, I . . . '

Essach took out his mobile telephone and keyed in Flora's mobile. 'Detective Inspector Essach Wangdula here. Is that you, Detective Sergeant Hughes? Ah, good. Just a quick question. Has that search warrant come through yet, please?' He listened. 'Never mind. Shouldn't be long now. I'll continue to wait here. You know where I am if you need to call me. In the meantime, please wait for my call. Thanks.'

Alan Lancashire stared at Essach briefly, not able to believe his own ears. Recovering his equanimity, he said, 'No need for that, Detective Inspector. I'll make those invoices available to you.' He picked up his desk telephone and dialled a single number. 'Helen? Will you please abandon what you are doing and bring me copies of all the decorating work carried out at 25 Friendship Road? Ealing. No, not this afternoon. Now, please. Immediately. I insist. Yes, immediately. Yes. Well print them off. It's easy enough. Thank you.'

'They'll be here soon, Mr, er, Detective Inspector. I never asked if you'd like a cup of coffee. We've had ours. We start at eight o'clock and have coffee at 10.30.'

Essach let him waffle on. He'd got Alan Lancashire on the run. He was rattled. Essach had fooled him into thinking that the search warrant was for use to obtain the invoices. Alan Lancashire had met his match.

'Yes, I think you'd better make that two, please, Yvonne.'

The coffee and invoices arrived together. Yvonne gave Essach a curious look. Helen gave him a withering look.

Essach looked through the invoices carefully.

Restoring the first stair flight lower knop which was found to be loose. Filling the woodworm hole in the newel post at the top of the same flight. Filling of an open joint between first floor landing skirting and the staircase stringboard. Rubbing down of all paintwork, applying undercoat and two coats of gloss paint as per specification.

Essach speedily perused the remainder of the invoices to divert any possible suspicions which Alan Lancashire might develop about the part which had really interested him.

'All seems to be as we expected, Mr Lancashire. Thank you for your co-operation.'

Alan Lancashire gave an almighty sigh of relief.

Essach downed the last of his coffee. 'Do you mind if I make one last phone call, Mr Lancashire?'

'As long as it does not involve my firm, Detective Inspector Wangdula, you can do as you like.'

Essach made the call on his mobile to Flora. 'Wangdula here. What is the up-to-date position, please? Ah, it's there. Good! As in all of the most popular television police shows, go, go, go! I'll join you shortly.' He snapped his mobile shut. 'Thank you, Mr Lancashire. You've been most helpful.'

Alan Lancashire gave Essach a lopsided and wrinkled sort of smile and escorted him to the front door. Essach could see through his rear view mirror that Alan Lancashire stayed on the front doorstep until he turned the corner towards Ealing.

By the time Essach reached 25 Friendship Road, the drive of the house was filled with police vehicles, and so he drove past the ubiquitous group of curious onlookers, and parked his car further along the road. He telephoned headquarters to have the original search warrant brought post-haste to 25 Friendship Road by a police motorcyclist. He walked past the constable keeping watch at the entrance to the drive, showing his warrant card, and again to the constable at the front door.

He barely had time to take in what was taking place before a WPC escorted Mrs Bullock out of the house. 'Just taking her to the hospital,' mouthed the WPC.

Essach felt an ice-cold finger run down his spine. Then realization came: Mrs Bullock wasn't being carried out on a stretcher; she hadn't had a heart attack. She was more likely to be on her way to the maternity ward. Her daughter had gone into labour. Well, he thought, that was no bad thing, considering what the SOCO team had come to do to her house.

'Ah, there you are, sir.' Flora looked composed. 'Work has started on the newel post and skirting, sir. And officers are in the garden with sieves to see what they can find, if anything, where the heathers are . . . ' she corrected herself ' . . . were planted.'

Essach shielded his almond eyes against the SOCO team photographer's spotlights. 'Seventeen steps. Old Mr Swindell-Banks never stood a chance falling down that flight of stairs.' Essach noted an abundance of protective sheets covering the hall floor and stairs.

Flora saw that the photographer had started to video the removal of the bottom knop which revealed a hole in the newel post wide enough for the head of a two inch nail to pass through. Essach watched with her. They faced each other and signalled thumbs up. The SOCO operative scraped wood dust from the hole into an evidence envelope.

'He's already taken photographs of the newel post at first floor level and of the skirting.' Flora added, 'sir' for the sake of police presence around them.

'I do hope that Mrs Bullock is all right.'

'Quite frankly, I think that her daughter going into labour has given her something important to think about for once. She'll be in good spirits once her grandchild is born, and both mother and baby are fine.'

'Until, that is,' remarked Essach, 'it is confirmed that a murder took place in her new home.'

'Well, she's already got her own back.'

Essach frowned.

'She's locked the kitchen door!' They both laughed.

'I know how to cheer her up.' A cheerful

smile enveloped Flora's face. 'We'll tell her that she has been blessed, that this house has brought good fortune into the Bullock family.'

'Why not? It is as tactful as anything I could think of.'

'Probably more so,' said Flora tactfully, under her breath.

They followed the photographer upstairs to where they could observe proceedings from the first floor landing by looking over the balustrade. One of the SOCO team had been gently sandpapering the side of the newel post opposite the skirting. They heard her give out a sigh of satisfaction. She beckoned the photographer to video her final revealing of a stopped hole in the side of the newel post. She picked up a small tool from beside her, put there in readiness, no doubt, for this stage of the operation. She gently screwed into the stopped hole, carefully catching the filling until no more came out. Looking over the stair-rail she gave a smile of satisfaction at the stream of thin dust falling from the bottom of the newel post.

'No need to doubt any more, sir. That's how she did it,' observed Flora.

They continued to watch as a length of thin wire was threaded into the small hole in the side of the newel post, and fed, inch by inch, until the end of it emerged from the larger hole in the bottom of the newel post in the hall. The end of a reel of garden twine was then attached to it and pulled upwards through the smaller hole in the first floor newel post.

The photographer then turned his attention to the skirting board opposite. The female SOCO operative joined a male colleague at the skirting board. At the angle where it changed direction to run downwards alongside the stairs, they both tapped home a wide but thin chisel on each side of where the skirting and stringboard joined. At a nod from the male SOCO they gently eased the timbers towards themselves. Alternately, gently tapping the chisels deeper behind the timbers, and easing them out, they were, eventually, able to see and video what was behind. The female SOCO operative beckoned for Essach to see what they'd found.

He gave a gasp of surprise, and then looked closer. 'Well, I never expected that,' he remarked. 'Detective Sergeant Hughes, I want you to see just how clever our murderer is.'

Flora took Essach's place. 'Well, well. She took no chances,' she remarked, as she took in the thin sliver of razor blade fixed to the inside of the stringboard at the joint. She turned to the female SOCO operative. 'Glued on?'

'Almost certainly. Ensured that the twine was severed when pressure was put against it. Too late by then. No saving yourself.' She found a long pair of tweezers and fished behind the stringboard. She held up a two-inch nail around which was knotted green garden twine.

Essach clapped his hands in the air, making everyone jump. 'I knew it. I just knew it. Now if the end of that twine knotted around the nail matches up with the length we found in Adrian Hill's survey file, we have proof, absolute proof.'

'And if one of the ends matches with an end of the ligature around Adrian Hill's neck? Why, that would be a bonus.' Flora smiled. 'However, we mustn't hold our breath.'

'Now to test your theory, Detective Inspector.'

Essach looked expectantly at the male SOCO operative. He produced a two-inch steel nail from an evidence envelope. 'We tie this to the twine protruding from the bottom of the newel post. Then we gently pull the twine until it comes to a stop inside the hollowed out newel post and stretch the twine across the top of the stairs to form a tripwire. We tie the nail we've just found to the other end of the twine, and, ah!'

Essach noticed that the female SOCO operative had been gently removing the filling from the joint in the skirting, again saving the stopping as material evidence, as her colleague talked. The male operative joined her in pushing the skirting and stringboard back into position as far as was possible. That done, the female operative took the nail, and, judging the length of twine needed to cross the top of the stairs, tied the twine to the second nail. She lowered the twine through the now open woodwork joint, and gingerly placed it against the razor blade edge.

The male operative stood two stairs down and his colleague leaned forward to place her hands on his shoulders. He, in turn, held his hands firmly against her waist.

'Looks as though they've already thought this out and have been rehearsing, sir.'

The male operative looked up at Flora and Essach to where they stood on the landing. He grinned in appreciation of Flora's astuteness. His colleague checked that the photographer was videoing them. She then pushed her foot forward, as if about to proceed downstairs. The twine kinked at her ankle and immediately snapped; both ends disappeared. There were two almost simultaneous 'clunk' sounds as both nails dropped.

It was obvious, even though she'd been expecting it to happen, that the female operative would have fallen down the stairs, as Mr Israel Swindell-Banks had done. Fortunately for her, she and her colleague had prepared themselves for that eventuality. She straightened up.

Both Essach and Flora applauded, to be joined by the photographer and police who'd witnessed the experiment.

The two SOCO operatives gave small mock bows in appreciation.

Essach and Flora left the SOCO team to complete their investigations by carefully removing the sliver of razor blade then clearing up and leaving the sites of their activities as spotlessly clean as possible.

Forgetting Mrs Bullock had locked it, Essach tried the kitchen door handle, sighed and made for the front door. A Goliath-sized policeman clad in protective leather jacket and over trousers filled the front doorway. 'Detective Inspector Wangdula, sir?'

Essach acknowledged that he was.

'Please sign here, sir.' Essach obliged. The policeman handed an envelope to Wangdula, before taking his departure. 'Thank you,' Essach called after him.

'We'll have to go around the side of the house to get to the rear garden,' explained

Flora. They were just about to proceed when they heard a voice yell, 'Stop, Detective Inspector.'

Essach looked towards the drive entrance where the policeman on duty had his arms outstretched barring access to Stanley Parton.

'This constable will neither allow me to come to my clients' house nor will he agree to find you and ask your permission for me to enter my clients' property.'

'Sorry about that, Mr Parton. The constable would be in dereliction of his duty if he left his post,' called Essach.

'He could just as easily have used his mobile phone or radio to contact you!'

Essach and Flora walked down the drive. Stanley Parton had flecks of foam at the corners of his mouth. 'You came to see my authorization to make a search of Mr and Mrs Bullock's house and gardens, didn't you, Mr Parton? Well, here it is.' Essach took the original search warrant from the envelope which he held in his hand and gripped it firmly while holding it out for the solicitor to read.

Stanley Parton moved his hand as if to take the search warrant from the detective.

Essach moved his hand back. 'Just read it, please, Mr Parton.'

'Alright, I've read it. Now let me come inside and see what damage you've done.'

'No, Mr Parton. When the SOCO team have completed their investigation I'll let you know. In the meantime, please do not obstruct the police while in pursuit of their inquiries.' He turned to the constable on duty, 'Good work, Constable. Thank you.' Then to Flora, 'Come, Detective Sergeant Hughes. We haven't finished here by a long chalk, yet.' He called back over his shoulder, 'Don't worry about the damage and cleaning up, Mr Parton, it is all part of the SOCO team's remit.'

They found their way to the heather garden. A member of the white clad SOCO team was busily sifting soil, and a colleague was carefully using tweezers to remove something from the sieve.

Set aside from the mound of soil were scraps and fragments of cardboard. Essach and Flora, without touching, could see familiar features of buildings. A part doorway here, a window corner there, a complete chimney stack, areas of brickwork and roof tiling, all charred around the edges. Essach signalled for them to stop.

'Thanks. You've done well. That's all we need for our purposes.'

The SOCO operative put down the sieve,

pulled his face mask down. 'You are sure?'

'Absolutely.' Essach gulped. 'If you could just restore the heather bed to how it was — more or less, that is — I'd be grateful. Oh, and bag those fragments up, please. We shall need those to support our opinion of the motive which led to the murder.'

The two detectives returned to the front of the house where they were out of the way of the SOCO team and supporting constables. 'I'm surprised that we haven't seen Mr Bullock,' remarked Flora.

'Now that is a real worry,' replied Essach.

They watched as the SOCO team in the house came out carrying rolled up dust sheets, spotlights, tool cases and evidence containers. They were replaced by a team carrying vacuum cleaners, brushes and dustpans and plastic carriers containing dusters and other household cleaning equipment. Not until they had completed their work did Essach telephone Stanley Parton. While they waited for the solicitor to arrive, Essach and Flora advised the constable on duty at the entrance to the drive to expect him and to allow him to pass. They then went to the heather garden.

As far as they could see, the heathers were in more or less the same place as before the SOCO team commenced work. 'The team

201

photographer would have taken shots,' remarked Flora.

'Was there really any need to replant the dead heathers?'

'They couldn't win either way,' remarked Flora. 'I'd say that it was the prudent thing to do.'

Essach shook his head in disbelief. 'Kysoh.'

'What's that? Tibetan? What does it mean, Essach?'

'It is my acronym for Keep Your Sense Of Humour.'

'Of course. That's what you meant when you said it before. I must be becoming thick!'

'No. Just very becoming,' answered Essach.

'Ah! So this is where you are,' came a loud voice.

Essach and Flora jumped, and turned from the heather bed to see who had bellowed at them.

Mr Bullock had come up quietly behind them, accompanied by Stanley Parton.

'Hello, Mr Bullock. How is your daughter?' asked Flora promptly, before Essach had the chance to say anything less than tactful.

'Hurrmph. Well, Daphne is fine, thank you.'

'And good news, sir?' inquired Essach.

'A son.'

Flora clapped her hands, 'How wonderful,

your first grandson. Congratulations! Is Mrs Bullock here? I must go and congratulate her too. Find out your grandson's weight, the colour of his eyes, if he has any hair.'

'If you must. You'll find her in the kitchen,' Mr Bullock bellowed after her.

'Now, Detective Inspector Wangdula. You and your crew have a lot to answer for. My solicitor and I have been inspecting the damage caused to my home — scarred paintwork, skirting and stringboard pulled off the wall. My solicitor can confirm my allegation. You wait until this reaches the newspapers.'

'Excuse me, Mr Bullock. The SOCO team did pull back the first floor landing skirting and stringboard, and, please listen carefully, they restored it so carefully that you must have given it a hard tug to dislodge it again.'

'That's an outright lie. My sol — Where is he?'

'Not prepared to perjure himself, I expect. Photographs and videos were taken before and after every stage of investigation.' Essach turned on his heel and walked back to the house.

'Don't you turn your back on me.'

Essach stopped. 'Is that a threat, Mr Bullock?' He resumed his walk to the house. The kitchen door was open. Essach carefully wiped his feet and entered. Mrs Bullock was smiling and the worry lines had left her face.

'Look at proud mother and baby, sir.'

Essach looked at the photograph of the Bullocks' daughter, Daphne, and a baby with a wrinkled face.

'Six pounds, seven ounces. Isn't he just gorgeous?'

Essach thought carefully before speaking. Tact. Yes, tact. That's what was needed. He heard Mr Bullock enter the kitchen behind him. 'You've been blessed today, Mrs Bullock. In fact twice blessed.'

Mrs Bullock frowned. 'Twice blessed, Detective Inspector? How's that?'

'Your first grandchild, Mrs Bullock. Always a blessing to every family. And today we have removed all and anything to do with the late Mr Swindell-Banks's accident. That is the second blessing. In my culture that always results in peace and happiness for the occupants of that residence.'

Flora gave Essach a look of approval.

'I trust that, from our conversation in the garden, we will not be receiving a bill for the lick of paint, which is all that is needed, to restore the minimal, unavoidable damage. Such an attempt could spoil this auspicious day.' Essach narrowed his almond-shaped eyes so that Mr Bullock should be in no doubt as to his meaning.

'No, of course not, Detective Inspector. Now I expect that you and . . . '

'Detective Sergeant Hughes, sir,' Flora prompted him.

' . . . will want to get back to your respective homes,' said Mr Bullock, before Mrs Bullock could question Essach as to what he meant by his last remark.

'Just what went on in the garden between you two?' Flora asked as they walked down the drive towards Friendship Road, 'And why did the solicitor rush past the kitchen window without attempting to congratulate, or say goodbye, even, to Mrs Bullock?'

Essach explained. 'Nasty piece of work, our Mr Bullock. Wealth and power. Often goes to a man's head.'

'And what about the heather garden?'

'He never even noticed,' admitted Essach.

Flora laughed. 'Kysoh. I told you so.' She was still laughing as they drove off back to Baluster.

30

Essach was ravenous when he arrived at his police section housing flat. He had barely started to put the ingredients for an all-day breakfast into frying pans and under the grill when a knock came on his door.

Essach opened his door to find the five other residents of the block on the landing outside. Harold handed him a large, sturdy brown envelope. 'Came by special delivery this afternoon. Fortunately it was my day off and I was at home to sign for it.'

'Thanks. Come in.'

Harold sniffed the air. 'Bacon. Well, just for a minute.'

The five of them trooped in. 'Find yourself a pew each.' He looked at them. 'Shall I put some more bacon on? Might just about have enough to go round.' Essach loaded his grill pan with bacon and sausages, leaving his fridge decidedly empty.

'Sandwiches,' said Eric. 'Er, bacon and egg sandwiches,' he added, hopefully.

It wasn't too long before all five were tucking into sandwiches, and Essach was demolishing a plateful of bacon, sausage, egg and baked beans with bread and butter.

Essach had been aware that Eric had been hiding something behind his back as he entered the flat. As soon as they'd finished eating and drinking tea from a variety of mugs, Eric produced a sparkly silver wrapped parcel. 'As elected spokesman, Essach, it is my pleasure and privilege to congratulate you on your intended move into your own house.'

All five grinned at Essach. They knew his new address, Essach was sure of that.

'Can't keep a secret from the police for long, eh, Essach!' piped up Charlie.

'Anyway. We've clubbed together to buy you this small gift to welcome you to your new home,' continued Eric, and handed the glittering package to Essach.

'I, er — I, er, I don't know what to say, chaps. We all work in different departments and hardly have time to say 'Hello' and 'Cheerio' in what spare time we are lucky enough to enjoy. Thank you. Thank you, so much.'

'Aren't you going to open it?' challenged Michael.

'Oh, yes.' Essach tore the sparkly wrapping off to reveal a long apron with a picture of a bikini clad lady on the front.

'She hasn't got anything on at all on the back, Essach,' called out Phil.

Essach turned the apron around to find that it was just a plain fabric on the back. They all six of them laughed.

'Right. We'll leave you to it,' remarked Harold. 'Thanks for the sarnies.'

Essach shook his head when they'd gone. What a nice surprise! Everyone at headquarters would know his new address by now. He then spied the envelope which he'd set aside when Harold handed it to him. He opened it to reveal a letter from Messrs Pink and Black, keys and photocopies of various documents. The gist of the letter was that The Cottage, Pestilence Lane, Monument Heath, Baluster now belonged to him.

The letter went on to say that his solicitor, Mr Pink, was offered the orchard next door at no extra cost, which he had accepted on Essach's behalf. Unfortunately, he was unable to make contact with Essach, although he did leave messages. Essach guiltily realized that he had not checked his own mobile all day, as he was so involved with 25 Friendship Road, and so had taken with him only the mobile supplied by the police force.

Mr Pink's letter continued — there was a snag. Someone living on the orchard was claiming ownership of the orchard under 'squatter's rights'. The family selling The Cottage did not want to be involved, and so, rather than risk a lengthy case and expensive legal costs, they were assigning the orchard, and its problems, to the new owner.

'Thank you, Mr Pink,' said Essach out loud.

31

'I thought we were friends!' Flora snapped, as she stood over Essach at his desk.

He continued two-finger typing his report on yesterday's events at 25 Friendship Road.

'You didn't tell me you were buying a house!'

Interested ears turned in their direction throughout the open-plan office.

'The completion only took place yesterday, Flora, er, Detective Sergeant Hughes.'

'Ah, but you could have confided in me that you were actually buying it.'

'True. But I couldn't bring myself to tell you.'

'On account of the address?'

'Well, yes. I was going to tell you. Honest.'

'You deliberately kept it a secret from me.'

'From everyone. Just who let the proverbial cat out of the bag, I wonder? Anyway, ladies have their secrets! Why shouldn't men?'

'Feminine secrets are different from male secrets. Male secrets are just bloody minded.'

A chorus of, 'Oohs,' came from the officers in the near vicinity.

Essach realized, too late, that it was

prudent to keep your voice down when conversations were held in an open-plan office. Background noise in the office wound down.

'We had a good day, yesterday. Don't spoil it. I'll tell you all the details when we're on our own later,' said Essach.

Another chorus of, 'Oohs,' followed but louder this time.

'Hah!' Flora put her nose in the air and returned to her own desk.

A constable placed a report on Essach's desk. It read: *Forensic report on the twine found behind the first floor skirting board at 25, Friendship Road, Ealing, London. The twine exactly matched both the twine ligature discovered around the neck of the skeleton of Adrian Hill, and attached to the two-inch nail discovered in the file of the survey of 25 Friendship Road carried out by Adrian Hill.*

The twine discovered behind the skirting board was tied to a two-inch nail, using the same knot as that used to tie the first found two inch nail.

Both nails appear to be identical and were probably from the same source.

The two ends of the latest found twine were matched up with the two other lengths of twine. One end had been severed in a clean cut and which matched the free end of the twine found by Adrian Hill during his survey. The other end was slightly shredded indicating that it had been severed by pulling (which would require unusually great strength) and matched up with one end of the ligature found around the murder victim, Adrian Hill's, neck vertebrae.

The sawdust taken from inside the newel post at the property matched the sawdust on the twine found in Adrian Hill's survey file.

It is my opinion, based on the clear cut evidence, that both crimes of murder were linked.

Essach carried the report across to Flora's desk. He waited patiently until she said an impatient, 'Yes?'

'I apologize, Flora.'

'Huh?'

'I know that this report will interest you. We now have the evidence to convict Rachael Smith. Good work, and thank you.'

'So what happens next, sir?' Flora emphasized the word, 'sir', with as much sarcasm as she could muster.

Essach gulped with embarrassment. 'I have arranged to have next week off work in order to move into,' he gulped, 'Pestilence Lane. I've agreed with the super to leave you in charge of alerting all police forces to search for our murderer. I will keep in constant contact with you. Hopefully, it will not take too long to find and identify a six foot three or four inch tall woman.'

Flora looked at Essach with disdain. 'Ever heard of Long Tall Sally?'

'Er, no.' Essach wondered just where the question was leading him to.

'A shop, sir. Dedicated to stocking clothing to fit women of five feet eight inch stature and taller. There are a lot of shops which have a tall lady department; there are a lot of tall women out there. Still, leave me to it. You just go and move into your new des res. I'll keep in touch, don't you worry.' With that she pulled the forensic report in front of her and began to read. She waved him away.

32

Essach spent the following morning phoning the storage company in Bicester where his furniture was waiting for him when he needed it. The manager gave him the name and contact number of a van and driver. He contacted the driver and arranged to meet him the following afternoon to move his furnishings and belongings to his new home.

Then he phoned and emailed BT, an electric supplier, Baluster community charge office, his previous insurance company, Severn Trent Water and Royal Mail forwarding service.

He made a make-shift meal with what little was left in the flat refrigerator and freezer after feeding his colleagues two nights ago. He needed to empty them anyway, in order to leave the flat and its furnishings clean and tidy in readiness for the next tenant.

Afterwards, he wrote to his parents, and to Rowena's parents to advise them of his new address.

Rowena's parents wrote to him from time to time. Mainly just briefly, then with a longer letter when it was time to remember the date when their daughter had died. He had attended the church memorial service on the first anniversary of Rowena's interment. Essach was torn between completely cutting himself off from Rowena's parents, and remaining in touch. At some time in the future he was certain he would meet another woman with qualities similar to Rowena's who he would ask to marry him — if he hadn't already met her . . . He would never forget Rowena but he was uncertain as to how long he would want to keep in touch with her parents.

He went to the nearest post box and posted the letter to his parents, but, having second thoughts, Essach pocketed the envelope addressed to Rowena's parents.

Taking his car, he put in a CD of Techung's *Yarlung Tibetan Songs of Love and Freedom*. Very soon, the song, *Evanescent Love*, was filling the car. He drove to Pestilence Lane and pulled onto the gravelled front area. He took a quick look around the inside of The Cottage to make sure that all was in order, before walking along the lane to where he'd noticed the caravan amongst the orchard trees when he'd first driven past after viewing the property.

The main body of the orchard lay behind an unkempt hawthorn hedge. He came to the gap through which he'd glimpsed the caravan. Beside the gap was a stout post with a notice, enclosed in a clear plastic cover, pinned to it. He stopped to read. *TO WHOEVER IT MAY CONCERN. John Smith claims his statutory rights under —* Essach read that John Smith was claiming his right to ownership of the orchard — *by virtue of having been resident on the site for the last twelve years without challenge or acknowledgement of any dominant claim.*

A man aged about forty was busily picking plums. He was near the top rungs of a ladder about ten feet long, and filling a basket held over his free arm. Essach noted that he picked the plums carefully, so that the flesh would not be bruised.

The caravan shone with bevelled glass windows and chrome trim. A black Mitsubishi Shogun was parked on a gravelled area. Its rear doors were open ready for loading the cargo space. Several plastic crates filled with plums, placed one on top of another, sat beside large opaque plastic containers.

Essach called, 'Hello there. I'm your new neighbour.' He pointed in the direction of The Cottage.

'Welcome to my home. Humble it may be but I call it my own. Have a plum or two.'

'Thanks,' replied Essach. He walked to

where the man was rearranging plums in plastic crates. 'I'm Essach Wangdula. I shall be moving in permanently tomorrow.'

They shook hands. 'I'm John Smith.' He offered Essach a basket containing Victoria plums. Essach took one.

'Take a few. They're delicious.'

'Thanks.' Essach took three. 'I've just bought The Cottage. With it I've been given the title to this orchard. Is it you who has made a claim to squatter's rights?'

'Yes, that's me,' admitted John Smith, as he polished a plum on the seat of his trousers before biting into the juicy flesh.

Essach was just about to polish one of the three plums he'd taken in the same way, and then realized that he was wearing a decent charcoal suit. Instead he rubbed it between the palms of his hands. 'Do you mind telling me what evidence you have that you have lived on this orchard without being challenged for, what is it, twenty years? You don't look old enough for a start.'

'Twelve years, prima facie, twenty years absolute. And I'm 38.'

'Yes, but what evidence?'

'I can do better than evidence, I've got proof.'

'What proof?' Essach spat his plum stone into the orchard grass.

'Now, wouldn't you like to know. I'll reveal my proof before the judge on the day my hearing goes to court. Will you be contesting me?'

'Perhaps. I don't know yet. You have witnesses?'

'Oh yes. I've got witnesses. Chiefly Jack. Oh, yes,' he laughed, 'Jack will be an important witness.'

'Huh,' retorted Essach. He turned on his heel and walked away.

'Enjoy my plums,' John Smith called after him.

33

Essach had roughly cleaned the flat, and packed all but the minimum he would need the next morning. He'd then set the alarm clock for six o'clock. Consequently, he was on the road before seven o'clock and at The Cottage soon after. He moved his clothes, tinned foods and other belongings into his new home. Lastly, he hung the apron he'd been given by his colleagues on the kitchen door.

He had put on an old shirt and faded trousers in readiness to help the van driver with the removal. He felt only just respectable. He parked his car so that it would not be in the way of the removal van. Making sure that he had money and credit cards on him, Essach walked back the fifty yards along Pestilence Lane to Tom Knocker railway station. He knew from the timetable he'd copied from his laptop that there should be a train from Warwick to Bicester at 7.40.

Essach heard the train whistle as it approached the station and so, self-consciously, put his hand out to indicate to the driver to stop. He was the only person on the platform. While

Essach boarded the train, the driver came onto the platform and turned a key in a tall clock standing against the wall of the station house. A light was on in the old station master's house. Essach felt sure that someone was living there. Sounding the train whistle, the driver edged the train across the unmanned level crossing.

The ticket collector looked at Essach oddly when he asked for a single to Bicester. Well, thought Essach, if anything happens to me, and he is interviewed, he'll remember me for two reasons. One, that I am, to him, a foreigner, who he'd never seen before, and two, I obviously didn't intend to return to Tom Knocker station.

As soon as the train arrived, Essach walked along London Road to the Market Square and made a beeline for a café doing a brisk trade in all-day breakfasts.

Afterwards, he walked around the market stalls buying oddments which he would need in his new home. He was about halfway around when he heard the cry, 'Plums, lovely Victorias, juicy temptation. Delicious plums.' Essach walked past John Smith.

At a nearby stall he espied a thick book, titled *Encyclopaedia of Garden Plants and Flowers*. It was published by Reader's Digest. He flipped through the pages.

'Keen gardener, are you sir?'

Essach looked up to see the stallholder, a man with a ruddy complexion and thin white hair combed across his scalp. 'Only a fiver. Cost a lot, lot more when new. Never goes out of date.' The stallholder turned away to an obvious potential customer equally as old as him. 'Sorry, sir. I've not been able to trace another newspaper of that date for sale.'

Essach looked up from the book to see the man's disappointed face.

'And I so wanted to give it to my grandson,' he said in a soft lilting Irish accent. 'The young don't know what really went on in Northern Ireland. There is a big article on the troubles in that newspaper. I want him to read it and to never forget. Ah, well. Can't be helped.' He passed behind Essach on his way to the next stall.

Essach looked at the stallholder, inquiringly. Behind him came the cry, 'Plums. Lovely Victorias.'

'I sell old newspapers with interesting news or articles in them.' The stallholder pointed to an array of them, each in its own protective see-through plastic wrapper. 'I had this one about six months ago. About the Omagh bombings, you know?'

Essach nodded.

'Well, that elderly gentleman was looking at the newspaper and saying that he would like to buy it. When, along comes that joker on the stall behind you.'

' 'Plums, lovely Victorias'?'

'Exactly. That's the one. Nosily he looks over the old gentleman's shoulder at the newspaper. Something seemed to excite him. He grabbed it from my stall. 'I'll take that!' he yells. Then he slaps a twenty pound note in front of me and is off like a scalded cat. We both yelled after him but he'd gone.'

'How peculiar!'

'Since then, the old man tells me, he's approached him to sell that newspaper to him. To even give him a profit on it. He tells me that he's offered the joker double what he gave for it. Forty pounds, I ask you. Money which I would think he can ill afford. But he won't sell. Now, would you like that book? Before someone snatches it from before your very eyes?'

Essach gulped. He handed the stallholder a five pound note. The stallholder held it under an ultraviolet light, before handing Essach the gardening encyclopaedia, in a flimsy peach-coloured plastic bag.

Essach continued walking around the market thinking of Bicester's shopping potential for him in the future. It was such an easy train journey away from his new home. Then he found a public house where he had a fish and chip lunch. Keeping his eye on the time, Essach made his way to the storage facility and talked to the manager until a large white van arrived.

'Bert, this is Mr Wangdula.'

They shook hands. Bert looked behind him. 'This is the wife; she helps me.'

Essach shook hands with her too. 'I came by train, expecting to ride in the cab with you, Bert.'

'Tha's all right. You can sit between me and the wife.'

Essach hung back while Bert and 'the wife' emptied the storage crate. He looked at them objectively. Bert must be about six feet five inches tall, the way that he towered over me, thought Essach. And 'the wife' not much shorter. He felt a wave of depression. If Flora was right, and there were many women about as tall and well built as 'the wife', then it was going to be no easy task tracking down Rachael Smith.

The van was soon loaded and Essach sat between Bert and his wife. Bert took the M40 and drove north to junction ten where he turned off the motorway and headed for Baluster. Fortunately, Bert drove with windows lowered, but even so, the odour of sweat in the cab made Essach's eyes water.

He studied the couple as they travelled. They were both middle aged and hard working, from what he'd seen. Bert was clean shaven, while 'the wife' sported the beginnings of a moustache. Apart from Essach replying to curt questions such as, 'Now which way?' And his replies of, 'Left up ahead', 'Turn next right', no conversation took place between the three of them.

Arriving at The Cottage, Bert reversed the van onto the gravelled front drive.

'Now, you just tell us where everything goes and we'll do the humping,' said Bert.

It took surprisingly little time for the contents of a one-bedroom flat to be distributed throughout a three-bedroom cottage. Essach noted that it was 'the wife' who set his fridge-freezer in place. And plumbed in the washing machine.

Essach counted out the price agreed into Bert's sweaty palm.

'And another fifty,' said Bert.

'That's the price we agreed,' said Essach indignantly.

'For the wife,' replied Bert.

Essach became aware of a belligerently thrust out bosom as 'the wife' loomed over him. After all, it was she who had plumbed in the washing machine.

'You don't expect her to work for nuffing, do you?'

Essach sighed and paid up. He watched with some relief as the large white van drove away. He left both front and back doors wide open to blow through and dispel the sweaty smell hanging in the air. Meanwhile, Essach set about rearranging smaller pieces of furniture, making up his bed, hanging his charcoal suits in his wardrobe and filling drawers. Then he closed the front and back doors before undressing, taking a shower and putting on fresh clothes. Only then did he wipe out the kitchen cupboards, before finding suitable places for glass and china. He cleaned the electric cooker left in the cottage and arranged his tins of food on the cool slab of the pantry.

34

Essach woke early, disturbed by the five past six train rumbling into Tom Knocker's station. His sleep had been troubled that night, and so it did not take much to render him fully awake. Yesterday had been a long day, but something must have happened during it to disturb his subconscious mind. If he could just remember what it was.

Essach put his old clothes on again. The sky looked promising and there was much to do both inside and outside his new home.

His mobile rang at 8.30 just as he was finishing a tin of all day breakfast on toast. His heart gave a little jump as he read Flora's number on the small screen. 'Hello, Flora. How are things going?'

'Some news. But first of all I rang you to apologize for overreacting when I learned that you'd bought a house without telling me. Why on earth should you?'

'My fault really. Pestilence Lane is not the most attractive name for the place where you intend to live. I guess that I was embarrassed. Sorry. Mea culpa. I was too intent on buying a house without taking on a mortgage hanging over my head for the next umpteen years.'

'That's as good a reason as any, Essach. Good for you. But kysoh, Essach. Kysoh. We have a lead. Every police force in the country has been given details of the Rachael Smith murders. I was beginning to believe that she'd gone abroad, but we've had news of a murder in Slough which appears to be similar to Rachael Smith's modus operandi, and involves a very tall woman. Ed Wallace and I have picked up her file and are going there. I know you must be busy, but would you like to come with us?'

'Very definitely. You can give me the details as we travel.'

'We'll pick you up in about twenty minutes.'

As Ed Wallace drove, Flora turned her head to look at Essach in the rear seat, while she gave him the details. 'It seems that a Mrs Croft has been found strangled, and with a ligature around her neck. Sound familiar?'

'I am sorry to hear about Mrs Croft being murdered, but her death might very well be the lead that we need to trace our prime suspect. Go on, Flora, what else do the local force know?'

'It seems that a woman answering Rachael's description, except that she's brunette now, has been making inquiries in the upmarket area of Slough. She's been targeting neglected houses, and asking about the occupants. Reckons she carries out property repairs and redecorating at reasonable prices.'

'That's one good way of locating her next victim.'

'Something went wrong for her this time.'

'Like it went wrong in the case of Mrs Lilian Wilson.'

'Seems so, Essach. The Slough force say that the house has been ransacked, and Mrs Croft's body was found tied to a chair. She was well known locally as a miser, and reckoned to be very wealthy.'

'And so probably kept cash around the house. The local force are of the opinion that she kept a lot of cash.'

'Sounds like our Rachael!'

When they arrived at Slough, Detective Inspector Paul Hamilton had more information for them. 'Her magnetic trade plates, on the side of her van, gave her name as Thelma Oldprint, specializing in property repairs and redecorating for ladies who preferred a woman in slippers and not a man in boots in the house. Or something like that. At least it captured the attention and memories of local residents.' His pale blue eyes twinkled, but his mouth gave away his determination. 'We'll catch her. A woman in her thirties carrying out household repairs, who drives a white van, and is over six feet tall. Can't be many of that combination about!'

'Detective Sergeant Hughes tells me that you reported a ligature around her neck. Do you have a forensic report on that yet?'

'No. But I have seen it for myself.'

'Green garden twine, tied with a specialist knot?'

'Green garden twine, yes. A specialist knot? I don't know about that,' replied DI Hamilton. 'We'll have to see what the forensic report says about that.'

'May we three be allowed to make contact with witnesses who actually saw this Thelma Oldprint? Show them photofits? We are pretty certain she could be one and the same Rachael Smith, alias, Ruby Stone.'

With warrant cards at the ready, and a short list of names and addresses of witnesses, they spent the afternoon confirming what they'd suspected.

Flora and Ed Wallace returned Essach to his home. They all three agreed that Rachael Smith had a bolt-hole. It was now up to which force found it first.

35

Now what? thought Essach, on the following day. After the excitement of yesterday he was thoroughly restless. Still, it was a sunny day, and he should do something constructive with it. He wandered around the rear garden. He noted the climbing plants intertwined in and out of the wire fence forming the rear boundary between the garden and the railway. The right hand boundary was formed by a well established hawthorn hedge, neatly trimmed, no doubt, by the occupier of the station house. He'd have to go and make himself known fairly soon.

Essach turned his attention to the left hand boundary; the one between The Cottage and the orchard. Again there was a hawthorn hedge, but neglected and overgrown. He'd occupy himself by trimming it if he could find a pair of shears.

Essach remembered the brick built tool shed when he'd viewed the property, and that the contents had not been removed. He looked inside and found two pairs of wellingtons, one pair small and another, larger pair. He removed his shoes and tried the man's pair of wellingtons on; they fitted comfortably. Then he located a pair of hedge shears with a thin film of rust over the blades. He went to his kitchen and poured cooking oil around the centre pivot. With very little effort he had them in perfectly acceptable working order. A good rub at the blades with cooking oil and a brillo pad completed the exercise. He ran his thumb along the blades, shrugged to himself that they'd have to do, and set about trimming the lighter twigs.

As Essach made progress, he saw through the twigs that there was a wrought-iron gate leading to the orchard, and beside the gate, a large timber shed inside the orchard. He concentrated cutting the twigs and light growth in that area to reveal the gate. A drop of cooking oil on the hinges should get it to open. Then Essach spotted the padlock and chain securing it. It brought him back to the skeleton murder: Rachael Smith. Where was she? The public, by and large, had no idea of the complexity of police work in tracking down a murderer. The detailed SOCO examinations to find potential evidence, and then proof; the searching to find the culprit. But by dedication and perseverance most were traced and arrested. No doubt the Slough force were searching cameras in public places, looking for any sign of Rachael

Smith, alias Thelma Oldprint.

Then his thoughts came nearer to home. John Smith. Just what was it about the name Smith? He wondered which of the Smiths, if not both, had troubled his sleep. He came to the conclusion that it was John. After all, Rachael Smith was Flora's responsibility for this week.

Essach returned to the potting shed in the hope that he would find a hacksaw or preferably, a bow saw. He gave up searching when it became apparent to him that there was not one to be found. He sat on an old chair and removed his wellingtons, to find a large spider squashed around the sock covering the big toe of his left foot. It did nothing for him to see that that was the sock with the hole in the toe. He put his shoes back on after dislodging the spider with the end of the shears.

Essach washed and then changed into his charcoal trousers, green shirt and green tie. He went downstairs just as a loud knocking came from the front door. He opened it. A smiling postal delivery man stood there. 'Hello, Mr . . . ' he looked at the top envelope in his hand, ' . . . Wangdula. I'm Andrew. Did I knock too loudly for you? Only old Mrs Vickers was really deaf. She wouldn't admit it, but she was. She used to come to this door saying the same old jokes every day. 'Do you think I'm deaf?' and, 'I'm the Vicker's wife'.' He handed Essach his mail.

'Thank you, Andrew. Call me Essach.' He had a sudden thought, 'Er, may I ask you a question, please?'

'Go on. Ask.'

'Tell me, how long have you been delivering letters to John Smith?' Essach pointed in the direction of the orchard.'

'Never.' Andrew frowned. 'I never have to go further than here. I didn't know that anyone else lived along Pestilence Lane. Mrs Vickers never mentioned anyone else, but then, I don't think she went out all that much.'

'Thank you, Andrew. You've been most helpful. I look forward to seeing you again.'

Essach watched Andrew reverse his van, before driving back towards Lords Wood Road. He then discarded junk mail, opened confirmation letters, and one Welcome to Your New Home card from Flora. She'd written, 'With every best wish, Flora.' He placed the card on the mantelpiece in the lounge.

Essach could not bring himself to believe that John Smith had lived on the orchard for over twelve years. Now that the previous owner had left or died, there was no one to ask — he hesitated — except the occupant of the Tom Knocker station master's house. Essach put his jacket on and walked along the lane. He knocked on the front door.

'Who is it?' a male voice called out.

'Your new neighbour, sir. I want to introduce myself.'

'Want to borrow a cupful of sugar, more like. Go away.'

'Can I ask you, sir, do you know how long the man living in the caravan in the orchard, further along the lane, has lived there?'

'No idea. And I'm not interested. Now go away and leave me in peace.'

'Well! Thanks anyway, sir.'

Essach walked past The Cottage to the caravan and rapped on the door. There was no answer. The Mitsubishi was conspicuous by its absence.

'John Smith, are you at home?' Essach called out. As there was no reply, Essach walked around the caravan. It was supported on concrete blocks at each of the four corners. Beside it was a stack of plastic crates. No doubt there is a chemical toilet inside but I wonder where he gets his water from? thought Essach. Then he remembered the large plastic containers in the cargo area of the Mitsubishi.

He walked around the caravan a second

time, noting the two wheel clamps to deter thieves. Something had caught his attention but he wasn't sure what. And then he spotted what it was. There was a gap between two of the concrete blocks supporting one corner of the rear of the caravan. Not an over-large gap, but definitely wider than any of the others. Odd, he thought, before returning to his cottage.

Essach opened a tin of stewing steak and a tin of ratatouille, heated them in his microwave, and ate his lunch.

Changing into his old clothes again, he pushed the vacuum cleaner around the old fitted carpets; those would have to be changed fairly soon. He finished with a desultory dust around.

He made himself a mug of tea, and then took a kitchen chair into the sunny rear garden to sit on, while sipping the tea.

The realization hit him, it was so obvious. That is what had disturbed his sleep. When John Smith had alluded to Jack, he hadn't meant a person, he'd meant a jack for lifting and supporting, a car jack.

Essach went indoors and fetched his laptop. He balanced it on his knees. Why, oh why, would he want a newspaper over twelve years old? One which carried headline news of the carnage in Omagh? There was not even a hint of the Irish lilt in his voice!

He booted up his computer, found Ask Jeeves web search, and typed in, 'What was the date of the Omagh bombing atrocity?' 'Saturday 15 August 1998', came up as the answer.

Essach's thoughts raced. That's it! That's the date on that newspaper that John Smith bought. He didn't want it for the news, nor for any sentimental value. He wanted it to try and prove that he's been on the orchard land for over twelve years. I bet he has dubious friends who will be prepared to swear under oath that he's lived on the land for all that time. Well! He's almost there proving his entitlement to squatter's rights. And, and . . . that's it! He's planted that newspaper somewhere where he can produce it on the day of the hearing. That wide gap between the concrete blocks supporting his caravan! That's where it is. I'd swear to it.

Essach closed his laptop down. Now what is the best thing for me to do? While he decided what to do, he phoned Flora. 'Any leads yet, Flora? Slough come up with anything?'

'Nothing definite. Lots of suggestions which have all turned out to be red herrings, so far. Don't worry, if Rachael's out there, we'll find her. But — '

'I know. But you think she's gone abroad by now.'

'The super thinks so too. He's alerted Interpol.'

'Ah, well. I'm sure that you are all doing your very best.'

'I can hear an echo, Essach. Is it something to do with your phone, do you think?'

'Um. No, Flora. I think it is more to do with the furnishings of a one-bedroom flat in a three-bedroom cottage. Only one bedroom, the lounge and kitchen are furnished. The rest is empty.'

'Would you like me to come and help you? I could come this evening.'

'You will always be welcome, Flora. But really, there is nothing to do. Shall I cook a meal, or would you rather go out to eat?'

'A candle-lit dinner, Essach? How romantic.'

'Um. We'd better go out somewhere. I know. There is an Italian restaurant over in Southfield. What about us going there. I'll book a table.'

'Not in Southfield,' said Flora, slowly and deliberately. 'Perhaps somewhere else.'

'I'll see what I can find.'

'Be with you at about seven.' Flora smiled as she put the telephone down.

36

Essach rose early. He'd decided what to do about John Smith. As if he didn't have enough to ponder on — the murders, and Flora's puzzling behaviour last night.

Flora had arrived on time, and presented him with a potted yellow geranium, before she asked to be shown around his new home. Essach had seen her look at the vase of summer flowers beside Rowena's photograph on the mantelpiece. He had put Flora's card nearby. When they'd got to his bedroom, Flora had stopped dead. 'Didn't you buy a new bed?' she asked.

'No,' replied, Essach. 'This one's fairly new.'

'Yours and Rowena's.'

'Yes. We bought this one brand new when we furnished our flat.'

'Oh,' Flora had said, as she speculatively eyed the bed.

The rest of the tour was rather hurried to Essach's mind. Still, he considered that the Italian meal had been a great success.

★ ★ ★

While ruminating over last night's events, Essach had watched from the empty bedroom over the lounge. The window was not over large, but gave a good view of Pestilence Lane. His wait was rewarded when John Smith's black Mitsubishi passed his cottage just after seven o'clock. On his way to one of the local markets, no doubt. Also, to fill his plastic containers with fresh water.

Essach made himself a bacon and egg sandwich for his breakfast. His irritation at having forgotten to buy HP brown sauce was only relieved by what he had in mind to do today.

As he walked along Pestilence Lane towards John Smith's opulent caravan, he mused that he was almost getting used to wearing his old clothes. He carried with him his car jack, and a section of thick timber he'd found when rummaging around his potting shed. Reaching the orchard, Essach was relieved to see that the Shogun was not there. However, to make sure that there was no one on site, he knocked on the caravan door, and called out, 'Is there anyone at home?'

Satisfied that he was alone, Essach set the car jack on the timber, and jacked up the rear corner of the caravan supported on the two concrete blocks with the noticeable gap between them. Aware that car jacks had been known to fail, Essach quickly removed the top concrete block and set it aside. He gently removed from the top of the lower concrete block what he'd expected to find.

'Ah!' he exclaimed. The newspaper wrapped in its plastic cover. He knew that forensics could examine it. Help him. But in this case he had to help himself.

Essach returned the top concrete block to its former place, and then gently lowered the caravan back onto the blocks. He'd already considered that the thickness of the newspaper which he'd removed could be enough to slightly rock the caravan, if he did not replace its thickness, and so alert John Smith that all was not right. He must put another newspaper of similar thickness in its place.

Essach walked back to The Cottage and placed the jack and timber into the car boot. He collected some cash and drove to the nearest newsagent. Taking the newspaper with him, he had a mischievous thought. Looking along the top shelf of magazines, he chose a girlie magazine of just the same thickness as the newspaper. The newsagent had watched him as he took down and replaced several magazines before finding the one of about the right thickness. When he went to pay, the newsagent rolled his eyes up to beneath his eyelids but said nothing.

Essach returned to John Smith's caravan and placed the girlie magazine between the two concrete blocks. When he'd finished he gave the caravan a push but it remained rock firm.

Satisfied, he returned home, and thoroughly enjoyed corned beef and chilli relish sandwiches for his lunch.

Later that day, he phoned Flora and said how much he'd enjoyed her company last night. 'We must do it again. Celebrate when this case is done and dusted.'

'That could be quite a long time, Essach. Remember we have yet to find the elusive serial killer!'

37

Essach had a restless night, and so rose early. He decided to go to Bicester again and see if the book trader was there. Also, the surveyor had recommended that he treat the woodworm holes around the base of the WC pedestal with Rentokil. He'd probably get that in the market. He dressed in his normal charcoal suit, green shirt and green tie. He didn't bother with breakfast.

The 7.40 train deposited him in Bicester some fifteen minutes later. He found the all-day breakfast café he'd eaten in on the last occasion, and repeated that pleasurable experience.

Essach found a small can of Rentokil with a nozzle made to insert into woodworm holes to inject the fluid. Then he made his way to the bookseller's stall.

'What can I do for you today, sir?'

Although Essach was dressed more respectably today, the stallholder obviously recognized him.

'Would you give this to the elderly man who so desperately wanted it, please?'

'Good heavens! Wherever did you get that?'

The stallholder peered at the plastic cover; turned it over. 'I seem to recognize that plastic cover as one of mine. Better not to ask too many questions, eh?'

'I'd be grateful if you'd keep it to yourself, please.'

'And not let old 'juicy plums' know, eh?'

'Exactly.'

'He won't accept it as a gift, y'know. The old man.'

'Why ever not?'

'Older people are not like that. They have their dignity and pride. I know. I'll charge him two pounds for it. He can easily afford that.'

'Well . . . '

'You bought a gardening book off me last time, didn't you?'

'Yes.'

'Right. Have this one for free. Then I'll accept the old man's two pounds for the newspaper, and he'll have paid for this book in return. In effect he'll have received the newspaper for free. Though, of course, he'll never know that. Sound fair to you?' He put the book into a peach-coloured plastic bag.

'W-e-l-l. Yes. I suppose so,' replied Essach, trying to work it out. After all, it will have still cost the old man two pounds.

'It's a good book, that. Especially if you are

planning to lay out a new garden.' He turned to another customer, 'Yes, madam, how can I help you?'

Essach walked to a café and ordered a coffee. He looked at the book. The *Flower Garden Planner*, published by Jonathan Cape. He opened it. Inside were push-out shaped clumps of garden border plants, and pot flowers, which could be slotted into pages of illustrated patios and garden borders. It gave ideas of how to group and display them.

After wandering around the shopping centre, Essach found a homely café offering chicken in barbecue sauce with fresh vegetables or chips and peas. He resisted the temptation to have the fresh vegetables and opted for the chips.

The sky had clouded over by the time he returned home. A light rain was falling when he arrived at Tom Knocker Station and so he ran the fifty yards or so to The Cottage.

Essach changed into his old clothes, and applied the Rentokil applicator to the woodworm holes in the floorboards at the base of the WC pedestal. A chemical smell pervaded the bathroom. He leaned out of the window to get a breath of fresh air.

From there he could see the rear garden in its entirety. The shower seemed to have passed over. The lawn grass would grow even after a light shower. He noticed something in the centre of the lawn. A space, perhaps. Something had been removed from there. A garden statue? Or a bird bath, perhaps? An image of his father's concrete mountain came into his mind. His father had made it a feature of his tiny back yard in Acton. A reminder of his home city, Lhasa.

Essach went into the rear garden and looked at the place in the lawn centre. A galvanized iron watering can with a brass sprinkler was hidden from the house by a bright yellow single flowering poppy. Essach picked the watering can up.

Inspecting the bare patch in detail, he could see that the grass was missing, and underneath was old dry mortar. Something had stood there. It was the very place for a garden feature; a mountain, just like in his father's back yard. He'd think about it.

As Essach returned to the cottage, water sloshed about in the watering can. He upended it but no water came out. He unscrewed the brass rose and looked down the nozzle; something was blocking it but he couldn't see what it was. Cupping the end of the nozzle with his hand, Essach put it to his lips and blew hard. He heard a splash. Something had shifted under the pressure of his breath. He looked inside the can. A large slug with green, grey, black and thin yellow stripes, was slowly squirming in the water. Essach emptied the contents of the can onto the garden.

He went inside his home and booted up his laptop. First of all he typed in 'Techung', switched on the sound and selected *Tsomo-Princess of Ocean* to listen to. Then he set about looking for a gardener.

38

Essach telephoned headquarters and was put through to Flora. 'No leads, Essach.' He could hear the disappointment in her voice.

'We'll get her. You'll see. Someone, somewhere, knows where she is.'

'Do you really think so? I'm not so sure. When we were interviewing her bank manager, and Miss Church, neither volunteered the name of a friend or former colleague.'

'That's because we neglected to ask. What about the theatre that Rachael was connected with? I wonder if any of the members kept in touch with her. Or rather, did Rachael keep in touch with any of the members?'

'Would you have done, Essach?'

'No. I suppose you are right. Still, you never know.'

'I honestly have got nothing better to do at the moment. It would be rather good to have an honest excuse for getting out of headquarters. I'll see what I can do.'

In response to his telephone messages left with local gardening firms and individuals, several returned his call. Quotes on an hourly basis were varied. When Essach asked for addresses, two declined to give theirs to him. At the very least, his police training, and the many burglaries he'd attended, had made him wary of people who could be contacted only via mobile phone, and who wouldn't give an address. One gardener who gave his name as George, invited him to his house to see his garden, and his rates were perfectly affordable. Essach arranged to see him that evening.

Essach parked his car in front of a neat semi-detached house in Lode Hill. While waiting for Techung to finish his *Song of Freedom*, Essach admired the front garden. It was mainly paved, but with borders to three sides cushioned with bright flowers.

He walked past a moderate sized lorry with 'George — Your Gardener', and his mobile phone number on the side of the driver's door.

George's mother answered the front door. 'He is expecting you, Mr Wangdula. George is in the back garden dead-heading and tidying. Come through.' She led Essach along the hallway and through an immaculate kitchen, then through a conservatory and into the garden.

'Hello, Mr Wangdula,' George greeted him with a warm smile. 'I won't shake hands yet.

Please feel free to walk around the garden while I go inside and wash. I get myself so engrossed in gardening that I completely forget the time.'

Essach walked around the garden and wondered if his could ever become as neat and colourful as George's. He shuddered at the thought of the condition of his lawn compared to the gardener's. Suitably impressed, he arranged for George to come and see his garden at eight o'clock the following morning.

On his way home, Essach stopped at a Chinese restaurant for a takeaway.

⋆　⋆　⋆

George knocked on Essach's front door promptly at eight o'clock, as arranged. Essach showed him around.

George asked, 'Do you have any preference for shrubs and plants, Mr Wangdula? As you can see, some of the shrubs have died and need replacing to keep the balance.'

'Ah! I know nothing at all about gardening, George. Also my job keeps me occupied at all sorts of odd hours. I rather hoped that you could come on a regular basis. Tame and maintain it.'

'Agreed, Mr Wangdula. I'll probably come

three times a week until I have the borders under control, and the lawn looks like a lawn.'

'Would you think it possible for me to have a mountainlike ornament at the centre of the lawn? My father had one, and I'd like one too. There has been something there. See that bare patch.'

'Sounds feasible, Mr Wangdula. Let me think about it. It might be a better idea to restore the lawn to one complete sward and have the mountain ornament surrounded by raked gravel, somewhere nearby, in the Japanese style.'

Essach gave George a key to the side gate, and agreed for him to leave a note of his charges beneath the watering can and collect his money from the same place.

Flora telephoned Essach. 'I spent yesterday evening at the Little Theatre talking to everyone connected with it. No one has heard from, or had any contact with, Rachael Smith, for the last six or seven years. No leads there, I'm sorry to say.'

'Thanks, Flora, you've done your best. I'll see you on Monday.'

Left to his own devices, Essach thought, What more can we do? There must be something. He went into the overgrown garden and picked several pungent orange flowers. He was almost certain that they were marigolds. He replaced the fading flowers in the vase beside Rowena's photograph with them. Then he realized what he'd just done: flowers to show respect to the dead; that's what Rachael Smith would be doing, surely?

'Oh what a fool I've been!' yelled Essach, and was glad that he had no nearby neighbours. That's what has been nagging me at the back of my mind. Rachael Smith has not left England. She will remain close to her father's grave. Her distorted love for him has been so strong that she has killed to get the money to keep him in comfort throughout his illness. And it looks as though she's either angry with her life, or has developed a liking for money and killing!

But where is her father buried? Where he lived, here in Baluster is the most likely place. In Lode Hill Cemetery. Essach wasted no time in driving to the burial ground. The gate keeper directed him to the cemetery office. Once there it did not take him long to produce his warrant card and to introduce himself at reception. He was shown to the manager's office.

'Mr Wangdula. Please do come in. I'm Celia Renfrew. How can I be of help?' An efficient looking lady in her middle fifties welcomed him. A neat black trouser suit and white blouse, complemented her pristine white hair.

Essach explained that he was looking for the grave of a Mr Joseph Peat. All that he could tell Mrs Renfrew was that he'd died probably between eighteen months and two years ago. He was offered a cup of tea while the staff conducted a search.

Presently Mrs Renfrew returned. 'We've found the late Joseph Peat. He's buried beside his late wife, Gladys, in a double grave. Plot number 11230 in the south section. I'll get Mr Sewell, the security guard to bring his golf buggy around and take you there.' She made a call on her mobile phone. 'He'll be here in two or three minutes.'

True to the cemetery manager's word, a golf buggy drew up at the reception entrance. 'I'll leave you in the capable hands of our Mr Sewell. Please do return and confirm that you've found the grave which you are looking for.'

Essach climbed into the passenger seat. 'Len Sewell. Everyone calls me Len.' They shook hands. 'I gather that you're with the police.'

'Detective Inspector Essach Wangdula, attached to Baluster crime squad. Len, I'd be grateful if my visit here could be treated with the utmost confidence.'

'If you wants it to be kept secret, Mr Wangdula, consider it done. I've learned a lot from my late fellow citizens here.' He waved his free hand in the direction of gravestones as far as the eye could see. 'They all keep their secrets.' The buggy gently made its way past the fingerpost which directed its reader towards the south section. 'Just like them, I'll take mine with me to the grave.'

Within a relatively short time, Len Sewell drew the buggy to a halt beside an attention compelling gravestone. It was as wide as a king-size bed. The white marble headstone recorded the names of the occupants in embedded lead lettering.

JOSEPH WILLIAM PEAT AND
GLADYS HILDA PEAT.
They were as dear to me, as life could be
And both crossed, alone, the sapphire sea
Why should I, then, fear the distant shore
Since those I loved have gone before.
Their daughter, Rachael

The whole of the grave was covered in white marble slabs with hardly a knife's width between them. Essach noted that the white marble slabs and the surrounding kerb gently sloped towards the foot of the grave.

Len Sewell noted Essach's frown. 'The

rain, which we have frequently, in case you hadn't noticed,' he laughed, 'washes the gravestone clean.'

'It looks very new,' commented Essach.

'It looks expensive,' said Len Sewell. 'Must have cost thousands. It's only been there a matter of months.'

'No flowers,' commented Essach disappointedly.

'No. Never seen any on this grave.' Len Sewell screwed his eyes up. 'Ah, yes, I remember her. Big woman. Taller than most men. Said that she may not always be able to get to her parents' grave, and that's why she had it designed that way.'

Essach turned away to hide the disappointment which must surely show on his otherwise inscrutable face. His eyes took in the adjoining gravestone. A grey marble car wheel, with dove wings protruding from either side. The sad monument to a daughter aged 13. The wheel told its own story of how she'd died.

Chastened by these individual reminders of the sadness of relatives who had suffered the death of loved ones, and which he understood, Essach asked, 'Please take me back to the office, Len.'

'Was it the grave you hoped to find, Detective Inspector?' inquired Mrs Renfrew.

'Yes, thank you. I don't suppose you have an address for Rachael, do you?'

Mrs Renfrew quickly found the all too familiar address in Brent which Rachael's solicitors, and her London bank had given him. Essach thanked her and returned home.

That statement of Rachael Smith's, that she might not always be able to get to her parents' grave, was ominous. It looked as though Flora and the super were right: Rachael had gone abroad. Her Slough victim had, hopefully, been her last. She could be almost anywhere. Now what? Wait for Interpol agents to locate her whereabouts? The very thought of a murderer escaping justice depressed Essach.

He went into the garden and sat in the sunshine. The sun warmed him. Life always seems better in the sunshine, he thought. He looked forward to George building a mountain ornament, similar to his father's.

That evening he decided to consign Rowena's photograph, together with the letter he'd written to her parents, but had never posted, to a drawer. He placed the yellow geranium which Flora had given him, in pride of place, at the centre of the mantelpiece.

39

'Nice to see you back again, sir,' said Flora, with Superintendent Salmone hovering in the background, and talking to another detective.

Essach sighed. 'Oh Flora, I found Rachael's parents' grave last Friday. In Lode Hill Cemetery. The ranger or security officer, whichever he is, told me that he'd seen Rachael at the grave. No mistaking his description that that was who he spoke to. He also told me that she'd had the marble gravestone designed to slope purposely to run off water. For the rain to wash it clean.'

'Not a bad idea.'

'Perhaps not, Flora. But he also told me that Rachael had had it designed that way because she told him that she may not always be able to get to the grave. You were always of the opinion that she had probably gone abroad. I hope not. I hope that her bolt-hole is not too far away.'

Flora shrugged. 'It's not your fault that we haven't yet caught up with her. I suppose you didn't get an address for her?'

'The same old one in Brent.'

256

'You'd better write up your report for the super, Essach. He'll find you another crime to detect. You'll soon put it to the back of your mind when you start a new case.'

'I suppose so.' Essach sat at his desk.

'Don't get up, Detective Inspector Wangdula. Did your move go well?' inquired Superintendent Salmone.

'Oh hello, sir. Yes. I'm settled in my new home. Thanks.'

'I overheard the gist of your conversation with Detective Sergeant Hughes while I was talking to Detective Inspector Wallace. Don't be downhearted. Keep it in perspective. You and Detective Sergeant Hughes have done all that could be expected of you. And more, if you went to Lode Hill Cemetery in your own time. I do know that DS Hughes went to the Little Theatre in her own time. Neither of you should make a mountain out of a molehill. In fact, you've moved mountains between you.'

Essach jerked at a sudden thought.

'DI Wallace needs some assistance with the case he's engaged with. I'd be grateful if you'd join him to help out.'

'Yes, sir.'

With a 'Good man', Superintendent Salmone walked towards his own office.

'That was kind of him,' said Flora. 'Essach.

Essach! What are you thinking about?'

'I was thinking about Rachael not coming to visit her parents' grave.'

'What about it?'

'If the mountain won't come to Mohammad, then Mohammad must go to the mountain!'

'What are you babbling about, Essach? Are you feeling all right?'

'Perfectly, Flora. Rachael's parents' grave is the mountain, and Rachael is the Mohammad of the saying. We don't know where to even start looking for Rachael. We must get her to come to us.'

'Give herself up, you mean? Fat chance!'

'What about an exhumation order on the grave? To dig up her father, who she has always unhealthily doted on. Unhealthily for Adrian Hill, Elsie Pridden, Mrs Lilian Wilson, Israel Swindell-Banks, Mrs Croft, and more than likely, her husband, Jack Smith. And I bet I know where he's buried too!'

'Where?'

'Beneath the pond Rachael dug out before leaving the family home. The peeping Tom burglar; I'm sure that was Rachael Smith checking that her husband's remains had not been dug up.'

'And are you proposing to get an

exhumation order to dig him up too?'

'Now you are being sarcastic, Flora.'

'Essach, have you any idea how difficult it is to obtain an exhumation order?'

'Well there's only one way to find out. Just a minute while I go and see the super.' Essach rang through and was told to go in straight away. He closed the padded door behind him. The padding was not sound proof enough to contain the super's yell of, 'YOU WANT ME TO DO WHAT?!'

A silence descended on the open-plan office as everyone in it strained to hear more, but the super had dropped his voice to acceptable decibels.

'What possible reason can you have for wanting to exhume your suspect's father's body? He's been dead for what? Well over a year? There can't be much left of him by now, anyway!'

'But, sir, we have no idea where Rachael Smith is. We could spend years looking for her, and still never find her. But if she thinks her father's grave is going to be disturbed, she will be disturbed too. It is logical to assume that she will make herself known, either through solicitors instructed to block the exhumation order, or, hopefully, she will come in person.'

'And you'll be there to arrest her?'

'Yes, sir. We really don't need to disturb her parents' grave at all. We just need to get the media to broadcast that we intend to open the grave. Desecrate it, I suppose Rachael Smith will call it.'

'No. I won't go along with it.'

'But, sir. We can erect one of SOCO's tents over the grave, which is standard procedure, anyway. No one will be able to see that the grave is not really being opened. It is the only way that we can possibly trap our suspect.'

'Hm. I see what you mean.' Superintendent Salmone frowned. 'I'd have to think about the implications, before agreeing to an application to the high court.'

'Please, sir. Who knows, Rachael Smith, under some other name, of course, could even now be housekeeper to another wealthy, potential victim. Or gaining access to another vulnerable victim's home as a painter and decorator.'

When Essach returned to his desk, Flora asked, 'How did you get on?'

'He's not going to give his permission. He's fobbed me off.'

'Ah, well then. Win some, lose some. Nobody can say that you didn't try.' Flora smiled. 'Don't let him get you down. Kysoh.'

'Good advice,' commented Ed Wallace,

who'd come to place a file on Essach's desk. The two male detectives looked at each other. 'You'll like this one. We're raiding a pole dancing club.'

Flora, who'd overheard, grinned.

40

It had been a long night raiding the pole dancing club, and Essach was still in bed when he heard the wrought iron side gate rattle. The noise woke him and so he got up. He opened the bathroom window to see George already at work in the garden. He had a small grass hook and was using it to take the lawn grass down to a level of a few centimetres.

'You're an early worker,' called Essach.

'There's usually a lot to do when I first take over a garden that's new to me, Mr Wangdula. Yours is not over-large and so I'll soon lick it into shape. Just a rough cut to the lawn before I mow it.'

'Have you had breakfast?'

'Well, yes. But what did you have in mind?'

'Bacon and egg sandwich, and a cup of tea or coffee.'

'I'm your man,' George called back. 'If you don't mind, I'll work until it's nearly ready. I'll need to wash my hands.'

Essach gave him the thumbs up and put two frying pans on the cooker.

They were sitting at the kitchen table

eating their sandwiches when Essach said, 'George. Do you have a computer at home?'

'Mm,' replied George, his mouth full of egg and bacon. He nodded.

'Would you do me a very special favour, please, George? I desperately want to catch a murderer and I need someone unconnected with the police to assist me to do it.'

'You're with the police?'

'I'm a detective inspector.'

George looked impressed. 'Do you know, I wouldn't mind helping you out. What is it you want me to do?'

Essach outlined his plan. George smiled. 'Oh boy, would I like to see you pull it off.'

Essach nodded his head. 'So would I.'

'I do understand. Just you leave it to me, though. What is it that you want me to do?'

Several days later, a column appeared in the *Baluster Post*.

BALUSTER POLICE CHIEF CONSIDERING HAVING BODY EXHUMED

It is understood that Superintendent Salmone is considering having the body exhumed of the late Mr Joseph Peat, buried in Lode Hill Cemetery. Inquiries are still ongoing in connection with the

263

murder of Adrian Hill, chartered surveyor, whose skeleton was found buried in a shallow grave in Southfield private park, and exposed by a fox, earlier in the summer.

It is believed that the proposed exhumation is connected with that murder inquiry.

We will keep our readers informed of progress.

Essach was called into Superintendent Salmone's office. 'Did you leak this item to the *Baluster Post*, Detective Inspector?' He pushed the newspaper in front of Essach.

Essach read it, furrowed his brow, and said, quite truthfully, 'No, sir. Have you asked the editor the source of his information, sir?'

'Oh yes. He's no help either. Pleading confidentiality. I shall find out, I promise you. As far as I am aware, only you know about our conversation on this subject.'

'Well, sir, it is not as easy as that.'

'What do you mean, not as easy as that?'

'Well, sir. Apparently, when I put the suggestion of obtaining an exhumation order to you, you yelled out loud, something like, 'You want me to do what?' and everyone in the main office heard you. In fairness to their questions, I had to tell them what I had in mind to try and catch my prime suspect.'

'Then I will have to question all of my officers to find the culprit, is that it?'

Essach gasped. 'Definitely not, sir. If you do that, your team will lose all confidence in you. I am quite certain of their integrity. None of them would stoop so low as to do such a thing, even if they agreed that it is the only way we are going to have any chance of catching Rachael Smith.'

Superintendent Salmone glowered at Essach. 'Well, someone with inside knowledge leaked that information to the press.' He was interrupted by his telephone ringing. 'Yes?' He listened. 'Tell them, 'No comment'. That was our information bureau. Apparently, the nationals have picked up on the news item. Now what am I to do?'

'Could I suggest, sir — '

'No you couldn't. Just go away. I need to think things through.'

'Yes, sir.' Essach left with a grin on his face.

★   ★   ★

Essach, facing the police information bureau video camera, said, 'In connection with an ongoing investigation to apprehend a serial killer, it has been found necessary to obtain an exhumation order. This order will be implemented on the tenth of this month in Lode Hill Cemetery.'

'Thank you Detective Inspector, Wangdula,' said the voiceover.

The video camera panned the south section of Lode Hill Cemetery, coming to rest on a unique white marble king-size gravestone. The lettering was pixelated. The video clip appeared on all TV channels.

★ ★ ★

Rachael Smith sat gripped with a mixture of outrage, and fear. 'I'll kill that foreign swine. He's somehow found out about me.' She banged her fist on the arm of her chair. Her thoughts raced. 'He doesn't know where I am. The only possible reason for him to disturb Mum and Dad's grave is to get me to give myself up. Well, I'm not going to do it.'

Rachael had a restless night's sleep, but, by morning she'd come to a decision. That slimy slug of a detective inspector would be her last victim. She intended to murder him before he could desecrate her parents' grave. She booted up her computer to find suppliers of the items she would need.

266

41

The days up to the 'exhumation' of Joseph Peat's grave would have dragged by for Essach and Flora if it had not been for the legal case, Smith v. Wangdula.

Essach had taken special care to tell Flora all about the impending legal case. He was not going to risk being hauled over the coals by her. Once was enough for him.

He was confident that John Smith had no real evidence that he'd squatted on the orchard land for over twelve years. What he intended to do was to try and pull off a confidence trick. Essach was being represented by Messrs Pink and Black, who advised him that he would not be called upon to give evidence. John Smith was conducting his own case, and so it was entirely up to him to provide irrefutable proof of his squatter's rights.

However, Essach had pre-arranged for George to provide a small mechanical digger for use later and to work on Essach's garden for all of the day of the legal case. John Smith needed to be booted out of the orchard for ever.

Soon after 2.30, Essach received the welcome telephone call he'd been expecting. 'Peter Wells of Pink and Black here, Mr Wangdula. You'll be pleased to hear that John Smith was totally unable to prove his case for squatter's rights to your orchard. I know that it would have been inappropriate for you to be here, but really,' he laughed, 'you should have seen both the judge's and John Smith's faces! The plaintiff had two witnesses who gave evidence. Under oath, of course. Both swore that they, and John Smith, had inserted a newspaper between the blocks stabilizing one corner of the caravan, over twelve years ago. You'll never guess what they found between the blocks!'

'You've got me there, Mr Wells. What did they find?'

Still chuckling, Peter Wells replied, 'A copy of one of last month's girlie magazines. A particularly fruity one. The judge was not amused.'

Essach laughed. 'Thank you. Are you still on site?'

'Well, yes. The judge has gone, but John Smith is still here.'

'Good. Will you please give him a message from me.'

'I'm intrigued. What do you want me to tell him?'

'First of all advise him that I am, in my professional life, a detective inspector attached to the Baluster police force. Secondly, that he has until six o'clock this evening to vacate the site. At that time, my contractor will dig out a deep trench across the gap in the hedge, to prevent further access or egress from my orchard. And last, but not least, if he is still on site after six o'clock, that I will apply to the court for an order confiscating both his Mitsubishi and his caravan to defray my legal expenses.'

'Er . . .'

'Don't say any more than that, Mr Wells. Don't perjure yourself. The message is from me, don't forget. As a final trump card, tell him to look at the mechanical digger in my front garden; that should convince him that I mean what I say.'

'Do you know, Detective Inspector, I shall thoroughly enjoy doing just that.'

Essach telephoned George on his mobile phone. 'Essach here, George. It is on for six o'clock. I've won my case. If John Smith is not off site by then, please phone me, and I'll arrange backup to protect you, as you dig a deep trench across the gap in the hedge. My solicitor is advising John Smith at this moment of what will happen.'

'Leave it to me Essach.'

269

* * *

Essach was relieved to see that no vehicle or caravan occupied his orchard when he arrived home. George was finishing piling the soil he'd dug from the ditch to form a bank as a second defence behind the ditch.

'Thanks, George.'

'No trouble, Essach. He was off site by five o'clock. I saw and heard him leave. He made enough fuss about it. Banging about and sounding his horn from time to time. And — '

'And what, George?'

'You're the proud owner of a girlie magazine, its pages distributed all over the orchard!'

* * *

On the ninth of the month, the Baluster SOCO team set up a blue and white striped gazebo-like structure to completely envelop the white marble grave. Two policemen carried out night watchman duty, just in case Rachael Smith saw fit to take some form of action: perhaps hide inside the tent.

From seven o'clock, policemen concealed themselves in the SOCO tent, and took up surveillance positions at the entrances to

Lode Hill Cemetery. They were all on the lookout for a woman some six feet, three or four inches tall.

Essach and Flora arrived half an hour before the main entrance was opened to admit the first cremation service, and took up positions where they could be easily spotted by Rachael Smith, if, and when she came.

'She'll come, she'll come. I know it,' Essach kept on saying to himself, as if it were a mantra.

Flora was equally certain that Rachael Smith would turn up. But she was apprehensive. A woman well over six feet tall would be spotted instantly. Surely she would never take such a reckless risk? She and Essach had discussed the possibility with Superintendent Salmone. The super had decided that she would come disguised as a man. After all, Rachael Smith had been in amateur dramatics; she would know how to act like a man — the long strides, the slight swagger of the shoulders, a hat to cover her auburn coloured hair. But she could not disguise her height.

Even as Flora's thoughts raced through her mind, two plain-clothes policemen were talking to a man who had stopped to place flowers on a grave lower down Lode Hill Cemetery. Her mobile played The Sailor's Hornpipe, 'Yes?'

'All clear. He really is a man.'

'I won't ask questions. I'll take your word for it.'

People were coming into the cemetery in greater numbers now. Singly, in couples, families, all ages, young and old. They seemed to be well spaced. No doubt some had come to attend a funeral service, and had taken the opportunity to visit the grave of a loved one, or of a relative's grave rarely visited. Amongst them, elderly ladies using walking sticks to retain their balance, or to help them climb the hill.

Flora's mobile rang again. Someone interviewed near the north gate. Again a false alarm. Flora felt comforted by her knowledge that she had a secret weapon in her handbag; ironically, it had been obtained from the amateur dramatic theatre where Rachael had spent her spare time.

Essach received the same calls on his mobile as Flora had received. He paced restlessly, stopping occasionally to read an epitaph, an inscription, and to think of Rowena.

Flora noted the group of people coming towards her, making slow progress up the hill. At the front, accompanied by a middle-aged lady, was a white haired woman in an electric wheelchair. A widow, no doubt, clad in black and with a matching hat and half veil concealing her sorrow. They were obviously all together, as no one attempted to overtake the elderly lady.

'My husband is buried close to that tent thing. I'm a bit nervous. You'll stay with me won't you, dear?' asked the lady in the wheelchair.

'Of course,' said the middle-aged woman, walking beside the wheelchair. She'd thought the old lady in the wheelchair had seemed nervous when she'd asked her if she could accompany them into the cemetery. Perhaps it was not long since her husband had died.

As the group approached, Flora noted the flowers across the lap of the lady in the wheelchair, and the two walking sticks loosely contained in a side wicker carrier. She heard their rattling as the group came up the path. Flora stepped aside to allow the group, consisting of the wheelchair, the middle-aged lady, two men and three younger women, to pass.

Suddenly, the woman leapt out of her wheelchair, throwing her flowers in Flora's face, and swinging her two walking sticks. One felled Flora, who screamed, 'Help!'

Before Essach could react, to help Flora, or to defend himself, Rachael Smith had cracked him over the head with her other walking stick.

The policeman taking his turn to watch over Essach, abandoned the spy hole in the blue and white tent with a yell, alerting his two comrades with him inside.

Rachael Smith was lying flat on Essach, her hat askew, trying to get her hands around Essach's neck. Before the three policemen could come to his aid, Flora snatched the tube of theatrical blood from her handbag, and squirted its contents onto her forehead. She threw herself beside Rachael and moaned, 'Help, I'm bleeding.'

Rachael Smith felt herself fainting at the sight. Her reflex action was to release her hold on Essach's throat, and, with a frustrated cry she keeled over.

'Quick, get her handcuffed,' ordered Flora. 'That's it. Now get her inside the tent, quick. Out of the sight of the public. Before she recovers.'

The three burly policemen lifted Rachael Smith's inert body and placed her on top of her parent's bed-like tombstone.

Flora knelt beside Essach. 'Oh Flora. What happened to your head? I'll ring for an ambulance.'

In reply, Flora gasped, 'Thank goodness you are all right. Just lend me your handkerchief, Essach. It's fake blood, but in the excitement, Rachael Smith took it for my blood. She cracked both of us over the head, but I managed, like you, to ride the worst of the swipe.'

Wiping the theatrical blood off as best she could, Flora followed the policemen inside the tent. 'Good work, chaps. One of you get rid of those playing cards, quick, before Detective Inspector Wangdula comes in.'

★ ★ ★

'You're never satisfied, Essach. You've got Rachael Smith under lock and key. You've got all the proof needed to put her away for life. What more could you want?' Flora looked at him askance, across the table in the Chinese restaurant.

'Where she's stashed all that money, that's what she won't tell me. It is all stolen and should be shared out between Mr Swindell-Banks's family and Mr Wilson.'

'Don't worry, Essach, they'll manage without it. Neither is short of a bob or two.'

'And then there is the question of where her husband is. I'd bet my bottom dollar he is buried beneath the over-large pond in the back garden of Rachael Smith's family home.'

'So you've said, Essach. Leave it.'

'If I could only get her to admit it. I'd get

an exhumation order and a digger in there like a shot.'

Flora reached across the table to take Essach's hand. 'It won't do you any good to get worked up. Rachael is not going to give you the satisfaction. I'll let you into a little secret.'

Essach's almond eyes opened wide. 'Oh? What is that, Flora?'

'I've persuaded Superintendent Salmone that you need a break, after the shock of Rachael almost strangling you. We've both been given Monday and Tuesday off.'

'But — '

'But nothing. Listen, Essach. I've rented a cottage at Parkmill, on the Gower Coast. You and I can explore The Mumbles, Oxwich Bay, Limeslade Bay, and many more. Oh, there's so much to see. It's years since I've been there. I'll be a young girl again. Pick wild strawberries on our walk to Three Cliffs Bay.'

'It does sound exciting, the way you put it, Flora.'

'It will be, Essach. The cottage is self catering so we won't be disturbed there. And I'll look after your every need.'

We do hope that you have enjoyed reading this large print book.

Did you know that all of our titles are available for purchase?

We publish a wide range of high quality large print books including:
Romances, Mysteries, Classics
General Fiction
Non Fiction and Westerns

Special interest titles available in large print are:
The Little Oxford Dictionary
Music Book
Song Book
Hymn Book
Service Book

Also available from us courtesy of Oxford University Press:
Young Readers' Dictionary
(large print edition)
Young Readers' Thesaurus
(large print edition)

For further information or a free brochure, please contact us at:
Ulverscroft Large Print Books Ltd.,
The Green, Bradgate Road, Anstey,
Leicester, LE7 7FU, England.
Tel: (00 44) **0116 236 4325**
Fax: (00 44) **0116 234 0205**

Other titles published by
The House of Ulverscroft:

COMING TO THE EDGE

Theresa Murphy

DCI Mattia is struggling with a case that involves politics, big business and a psychopathic killer. He's depressed: the combination of his current investigation into the murder of young girl singer, his rocky relationship with his girlfriend, and his infatuation with a sexy private detective are all having an effect. But as members of his team are attacked, it looks like he might be onto something. Will he succeed in clearing the murder victim's husband, whom he believes to be innocent, or will his police career end in ignominy and the loss of the woman he now knows he loves?

THE SECRETS MAN

John Dean

When DCI John Blizzard visits a friend in hospital, he is intrigued when an elderly villain in the next bed reveals much about Hafton's criminal gangs. These revelations attract a series of sinister characters to the ward. Blizzard wonders if they are seeking to silence the old man, but fellow detectives believe that the pensioner is suffering from dementia. It's only when people start dying that his colleagues take the DCI seriously. Blizzard faces a race against time to save lives, and must face a part of his past he's tried to forget — and with the one man he fears.

DEAD SHOT

June Drummond

Leading industrialist Trevor Cornwall was found dead at the gates of his daughter's estate. It was remarkable not only that he had been mysteriously shot but also that the murderer had already delivered an obituary notice to a newspaper. Then there was another murder. Were the murdered men victims of a crazed killer or someone who had felt wronged by these prominent personalities? This was to prove a baffling case for DCI Dysart and Dr John Thorneycroft and there would be many surprises before the killer was finally unmasked.